LEGISLATIVE BODY

By Joe L. Hensley

LEGISLATIVE BODY
DELIVER US TO EVIL
THE COLOR OF HATE

JOE L. HENSLEY

LEGISLATIVE BODY

PUBLISHED FOR THE CRIME CLUB BY
DOUBLEDAY & COMPANY, INC., GARDEN CITY, NEW YORK 1972

All of the characters in this book
are fictitious, and any resemblance
to actual persons, living or dead,
is purely coincidental.

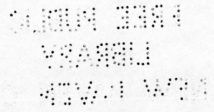

Library of Congress Catalog Card Number 76–186025
Copyright © 1972 by Joe L. Hensley
All Rights Reserved
Printed in the United States of America
First Edition

LEGISLATIVE BODY

CHAPTER I

RULE 1. *The General Assembly shall be composed of two houses.*

That cold afternoon they threw sod in the coffin-covered face of my shiny new and now lost friend, Sloan Link. The church was crowded, but they made a special place in front for Governor Bratewell and for us five legislators who'd been appointed to appear by the President of the State Senate and the Speaker of the House.

My name is Donald Robak, and I was one of the five. As a freshman legislator, I really shouldn't have been, but Ed Polsen, the majority leader, hadn't been able to make it at the last moment and had sent me on in his place.

So there I was at the funeral, although I abominate funerals. I suffered through it, feeling the sweat run down my back, despite the fact the church wasn't overwarm. Then we followed the funeral cortege to the cemetery in our loaned black Lincoln with uniformed state policeman attached.

At the cemetery I stood next to George Chapell, who's minority leader and a fairly nice fellow for a member of the Opposition party. He's close to sixty and continually suffers from a disease, inflamed nostalgia. He'd known Sloan Link

1

over the years and known him well. Each time the preacher, who was merely going through the right and proper motions, came up with a new attribute for Sloan, then George would nudge me and grimace painfully.

I stood stiffly and watched. Out of the corner of my eye, I saw the governor's driver, another uniformed state policeman, suddenly bend down and listen intently to his radio, and I got the feeling that something was up. I suppose I wouldn't have caught the movement or sensed that something was happening if I hadn't grown bored of the eulogies and sore from Chapell's repeated nudgings.

From what I knew of Sloan Link, he wouldn't have listened half as long as I'd listened. He'd not been a patient man, but he'd been, from both the reputation he'd acquired over the years and from what I'd learned of him, a hale fellow and an excellent judge of sour-mash Bourbon. He'd also been my seatmate in the state legislature. I was sorry he was dead, and I knew I'd miss him, but I was miserable being at his funeral.

They got over with the solemnities finally, and Sloan's distant relatives got into the front car and sped off. There were no close relatives.

I watched the governor's driver. He went into close conference with the governor, and I wandered over into earshot when Governor Bratewell caught my eye and motioned.

Governor Bratewell is a member of the Opposition also, but my law partner, ex-Senator Adams, thinks highly of him and worked for his nomination. I suppose he's better than the political clown my own party proposed, who lost ably.

Bratewell reached out and touched my shoulder. He seems to talk better when he's touching someone. He looked at the state policeman. "Tell Don here what you heard on the police radio, Charlie."

The state policeman eyed me dubiously, and Governor Bratewell loosed my shoulder and grinned.

"They were saying that they think now that this Sloan Link was murdered." He shook his head. "It wasn't on the police band. It was on a station from Capitol City, the news from there. Wasn't our people who said it. It was the Capitol City police." His eyes left mine. Obviously he didn't believe any news released by the Capitol City police.

"What do you think, Don?" Bratewell asked.

I shrugged. "I suppose it's possible. I sat next to him in the house. He got lots and lots of crank letters. You know he was coauthor of that tuition bill, the one that would authorize colleges to hire special police and then pay those police out of tuition hikes. That didn't help his popularity. He was also on a lot of other hot legislation—that new, tough anti-pollution bill, a shadowy cross-state power bill that no one seems to understand or want to explain and some others." I nodded. "I suppose anytime someone falls out of a window, then you run into questions. He drank, but I never heard him complain of vertigo."

Charlie said: "The radio said they found something in his room that indicated someone else was in there when he went out the window. The Capitol City police have been watching the room. Maybe they thought whoever it was would come back. That's supposedly why they didn't say anything until now."

The governor looked restlessly at his watch, losing immediate interest. "We better get on the way, Charlie." He nodded at me. "If you see your partner, Senator Adams, this weekend, tell him I'd like to have him come up or call me. I'd like to get him up in Capitol City for the last few weeks of the legislative session to act as a liaison between my office and the legislature."

3

"I'll tell him," I said noncommittally.

I watched him slide into the back seat of the Cadillac with the star-one license plate. Then I went back to the big Lincoln I'd ridden up in, which was star-two and had been loaned to us by the lieutenant governor for the trip.

George Chapell leaned forward in the car seat and looked at the grave site.

"Horse manure," he said softly. "They should have put him more in the sun. It's too shady there. Sloan liked to be out in the sun." He shook his head. "Ed Polsen told me that Sloan was going to Florida as soon as the session ended. He'd have blown all his money at the tracks"—he smiled, remembering—"and come back next time still against legalized gambling and a pari-mutuel bill."

I considered Chapell. He is a thin man with an ability to turn a nasty phrase. I placed his age in the high fifties, but he has a sort of residual handsomeness. I'd heard around the legislature that he used to be quite a ladies' man until age slowed him down. I know that he has a wife. I've seen that cold, blond lady around the halls, her eyes icy as she contemplates her domain. Either she never caught him in bygone years, or she let such matters pass. She has the money, I've heard.

I said: "Charlie, the state policeman who drives the governor, told me a minute or so ago that they're saying over the news that Sloan might have been murdered."

Four sets of startled eyes examined me, assessing that for political consequences.

"I heard that too," said our state policeman.

Albert McGuire, who was the house Speaker, looked pensive and said: "Maybe someone is bagging legislators."

I watched him. He is immensely fat and immensely able,

4

and he shares the fate of most men who hold big power—he is not liked by many for long.

"How's that?" Chapell asked.

"I mean nuts," said the Speaker.

Chapell watched him inquiringly.

McGuire shook his ponderous head. "I mean there's all these nuts hanging around the legislature." He nodded at me coldly. "Robak here represents about two-thirds of them. Marches, bomb scares, broken windows." He shook his head in wonderment. "Last week those three guys blew themselves up on the north side of Capitol City trying to cook nitro." He shook his head again. "Who do you think they were cooking it for?" he asked ominously.

"I've never seen a session like this one," Chapell said.

The two senators said nothing. I suppose they were concentrating on their own problems.

I haven't seen a session like this one before either, but that was explainable. This was my first, and probably my last, session. It had been a little wild, what with protest marches going on here and there, window-breaking forays in downtown Capitol City by riotous mobs of kids, state-flag burnings and assorted hangings in effigy. However, I was from Bington, a quiet, university kind of town, and so I was used to that sort of thing.

The state policeman drove on stolidly, ignoring the posted speed limit with dignified aplomb.

I sat back in the deep seat of the Lincoln and tried to sleep.

I was a state representative by a fluke. They hadn't elected a state representative out of Mojeff County from my party since right after the last civil war. When my county chairman had asked me to run, I'd run only because I'd really felt certain I wouldn't win. Besides, I'd had a few drinks when I was asked and agreed. My opponent was a grand old man

5

who'd served eight terms in the legislature and never made anyone mad. He had a fine smile, wore lovely clothes, and some wag reported solemnly that he'd finally found the men's room in the Capitol Building just the session before. He was an institution. His lowest victory margin had been something like two thousand votes.

I won by fifty-odd votes. When they filed the inevitable recount, I won that by more than sixty votes.

It was, as my law partner, ex-Senator Adams said: "Enough to shake your faith in the system."

So here I was: State Representative Donald Robak, now on sabbatical from the firm of Adams and Robak, Attorneys at Law.

The sixty-day session was half over, and the pace was beginning to quicken.

And now someone had maybe murdered my seatmate. It brought a queasy feeling, as if someone had walked on my grave.

Finally, I did go to sleep. My dreams were fortunately of a better, gentler world than the one I inhabited.

In Capitol City I reside at the Hotel Blue with many, many other legislators. The hotel houses us at really give-away rates because they pick up, at exorbitant rates, many of the lobbies and lobbyists who outnumber the legislators ten to one. The Hotel Blue is full of open hospitality rooms so that a thirsty legislator is never far from drink.

I was a thirsty legislator.

But first, to business. My room is on the third floor, and I made it up there via an ancient elevator that shimmied dangerously in the shaft. I opened my door and went into my tiny bath and washed sleep from my eyes and examined me critically. There I was, Don Robak, mid-thirtyish and no

6

real prize. I shaved and brushed my teeth for all the good it did, and then I changed from my dark, somber suit into odd pants and a sport coat. All of this helped a little.

Then I went out into the wide world of the Blue Hotel seeking drink and information and, hopefully, Judy St. Avery.

The law rooms were one floor up. The state's sheriffs and police forces combine to foot the tab for operating them. I walked up there. From quite a ways you could hear the sounds coming from the suite. I went on in and ordered and got a heavily poured drink thrust into my hand. A party was in progress, a continuous party. It had been going now for slightly over thirty days, and it was good for about that many more. Now and then the cast changed as people wandered away and slipped back, but the party remained a going concern. The rooms were constantly crowded with legislators, state employees, off-duty police and sheriffs and hangers-on. In one corner, now, I spied Ed Polsen, my majority leader, but it didn't seem a fit time to talk to him. He was in close, feverish conversation with a handsome, very young girl I recognized vaguely as a senate receptionist. From the way they were watching and touching each other, I thought they wouldn't last long in this crowd. Soon they'd move on to less crowded quarters.

Representative Fred Olean waved to me, and I slipped through the crowd toward him, relieved at seeing a friend. He's another first-term representative. He is a big, handsome Negro, one of seven serving in the legislature. He has a degree from Michigan State in Agriculture, and he operates a string of dry-cleaning plants and a large farm upstate. He's bright and able, and I like him very much.

"Hello, white man," he said. "You eaten yet?"

"Not yet, black man," I said, shaking my head and grinning.

"If you can stand more soul food, stick close. I've got a guy

7

runs a small loan company who wants to bend my ear and intimidate me a little. He told me to get a couple more. I guess he'd put up with a honky." He smiled, and it changed his fortyish face into something very pleasant.

We were insulting-type friends, and I grinned back.

"What do you hear on Sloan Link?" I asked.

He shrugged. "I was talking a while ago to one of the more friendly Capitol City cops. I guess they checked Sloan's room sometime after he went out the window—the amount of time varies from source to source. Someone had tidied up, but there'd been some kind of trouble in the room. Whoever it was in there got scared and beat it before the cops got there. Then one of the night maids reported she'd heard loud music coming from the room. When she knocked on the door, the music was turned down, and someone put on the inside bolt lock. She left. Her time on that would make it *after* Sloan went out the window." He looked around furtively. "There's cops all over. Where there aren't cops, there's newspapermen. Watch what you say. The newspapers up here don't like us, black or white, you know."

He was right about that. The first day of the session the big daily newspaper, the Capitol City *Enquirer*, published an enormous full-page cartoon showing a circus arriving, led by more than a hundred clowns. If a legislator looked close, he could maybe see a resemblance to himself in one of those clown faces. On that day they'd even proposed a resolution for us. Instead of meeting sixty days every year, they suggested we meet one day every sixty years.

"That paper could twist it up if they heard a man praying," Olean finished softly.

"Who'd want to kill Sloan?" I asked.

He shook his head. "I began conjecturing after I got the news and heard the gossip. There are a lot of possibles, in-

8

cluding your university kids. The best bet you hear about is someone hired by one of the outfits his anti-pollution bill would put out of business—a professional."

"Why?" I asked, puzzled. "Someone else will step in and carry the bill."

He smiled. "Not the way Sloan did. He was making the bill into a personal crusade. He had a real hard on for some power company that operates up there where he lived. I think he bought a farm a few years ago, and they made him pay for the transmission poles that went into it from their main line. It's a typical arrangement, but it made Sloan mad. You know how he was. That same power company built a big generating plant up there in his country and started operating it about a year ago. If the bill that Sloan proposed passes, it would put them out of business." He shook his head. "Say the word 'pollution' these days, and you bring all of them out of the woodwork. The bill had a damn good chance of passing."

"Maybe it should pass," I said.

He shrugged noncommittally. "Maybe."

"You hear anything about where he was or what he'd been doing on the night he went out the window?"

His dark eyes surveyed me. "Why the interest?"

"Call it morbid curiosity if you want," I said and grinned. "And he was my friend."

His voice was very soft. "Leave it to the right people, Don. Don't make waves up here." He continued to watch me, looking for something in my face. Whatever he saw there must have satisfied him that it was all right for him to answer. He sighed and said: "He went out the window about two o'clock in the morning. No one saw him come in the hotel. You can use the service elevator, and maybe, just maybe, no one would see you. He could have been out that evening, and then he may not have been out." He looked around at the crowd carefully. "No one's saying anything. He also could have been in some kind of personal or medical trouble and picked that way to dutch out. Until most of the bastards around here know for sure what it'll do for, or to them, you can't get them to even admit more than a nodding acquaintance with him." He grinned and pulled the old joke. "They say nodding."

I grinned back at him, liking him very much. He is a very observant and astute man. He has complete tolerance for the rest of the world. He doesn't hate me or eye me with suspicion because I'm white. I have the feeling that now, fairly late in life, he's on the verge of a big political career if he wants it. I also have the idea that he really doesn't give a damn one way or the other. Those kind make the great ones, because they can't be hurt or disappointed and so ring true without that falseness that the normal professional politician has. Professional politicians *want*. That want makes them less, makes them vulnerable.

Over his shoulder at the door to the suite, I saw Judy St. Avery glide in. She saw me eying her and smiled.

I said to Fred Olean: "I think I'll take a rain check on that dinner."

He followed my eyes. "Judy, Judy, Judy," he mocked, good-naturedly. "You have taste, Don. That's one nice girl."

"Sure," I said. "But she belongs to the wrong party."

He banged me briskly on the shoulder and strode away, and I went across the room and got to Judy. I'd now known her for thirty-odd days and had my first date with her only two weeks before. I got her a drink at the bar and got myself a fresh one.

"I was looking for you," she said. "George Chapell came

back over to the Statehouse, so I knew you'd returned from the funeral. I thought maybe you'd be here."

"I'm glad you found me. I was going to call you at home in a little while. I thought you'd already be gone by the time we got back, so I didn't come over."

I watched her. She is a lovely girl. You can almost visualize her in a skirt and sweater leading cheers for the proverbial State U. She looks about twenty-two and is eight years older than that. She has a son who's a nice little nine-year-old. She has an ex-husband who keeps a jealous eye on her when he can get away from whatever dolly he's hanging with currently. He's a balding, semipsychopath who found himself unable to leave anything alone after they were married—other women, booze, and finally drugs. He has a lot of family money that he's managing to squander. He fought the divorce. Now he spies on her and hates anyone who gets around.

I have every intention of getting around, and my greatest hope was to be number one on his hate parade. I like tall girls with gray-green eyes that stare straight back at you. Sometimes I get the feeling that she's waiting cautiously for me to hurt her also, and it makes me sad. I ignore the ex-husband. When he first found out about me, he tried calling me at the hotel at odd hours to annoy me. There's a regular, late-hour hotel switchboard operator. With a box of candy, I taught her his voice. When he'd call, she'd pretend to ring my room but wouldn't, of course. Pretty soon he caught on or got tired, I don't know which. So far, he hasn't tried anything physical. I doubt that he will. I'm as big as he is, and I'm not —last time I looked—hooked on anything, and I'm not—for a bonus—bald on top.

But you see, we have a problem, Judy and I. If I know about her, she also knows about me. She knows I was married and divorced young, while I was still in undergraduate school. She knows that it hurt a lot because, after a few drinks, I told her it hurt a lot. She knows I've had a problem making anything into a lasting affair since that time, and, sometimes, when she looks at me and is deep in, there isn't a speck of hope in her eyes for either of us.

She's told me several times that we are losers. I have to keep at her pretty hard now and then to keep her from really believing that full time.

It's worth trying. Sometimes I can get her to laugh and forget everything there ever was except the good times. When she lifts her head, and I see the long, clean line of her neck caught in that laugh, and I catch the sparkle in her green eyes and watch the mobile face made for happiness, then I want all of the good things for her.

She is something. And I've begun to hope crazily *that* something might be for me.

If she has a fault, it's that she's become a little afraid of life. She's perfectly willing to float helplessly around in the back eddies of living as long as the boat is strong, and she is a mere observer, but she wants nothing to do with actually getting involved in the action. I can make her shudder by telling her about my political campaign, about trying cases, about dealing with people.

She could have a better job. She prefers to work in the attorney general's office taking dictation from some of the more scholarly members. It pays well, but is low pressure.

She kids me about wanting to marry her, making it into a joke. I'm supposed to be trying to save the cost of a legal secretary. Sometimes, in the joking, the panic isn't very far away.

And so I wait.

She drank that first drink quickly, skittish in the company

of so many people. I watched her closely and got her another when it was finished. The whiskey started to relax her.

We danced slowly for a while to the music of the suite's free jukebox. Then, later, we went to her apartment and ate warmed-over roast and watched television. I played adoptive father to her boy, Alex, engaging in checkers with him, hoping she'd see that we genuinely like each other.

Then, unfortunately, not of my own choosing, back to the Blue Hotel and my own lonely bed. The kisses at her door had seemed warmer, less afraid.

I had hope, much hope. I dreamed on that.

CHAPTER II

RULE 3. *The lower house of the General Assembly shall be a house of representatives composed of 100 members elected for two-year terms.*

The first time I saw the legislative chambers I was much awed by them. That was a long time ago, more than thirty days. Now I was quite cosmopolitan on the surface. Underneath I was still the small-town lawyer in the state capitol and never really sure of what was going to happen next.

Albert McGuire, the Speaker, told me once that they'd last remodeled the chambers when they raised taxes, and there was some extra money. The job was done luxuriously. The new wing on the Statehouse where the chambers were now located was first class. They'd even made an office area of sorts for the members of the legislature. Those offices were only tiny cubicles with desk, filing cabinet and chair, but a legislator could say, for the effect it had on the old home town, that he had an office in Capitol City.

The chamber itself was much more impressive. The best experts had designed its cunning lighting and sound system, picked the artists for its murals. It's a warm room when it should be warm and a cool one when it should be cool. A rumor has it that the contractor, once a political wheel, retired to Florida after its construction and refuses to answer all subpoenas.

The furnishings are also plush. The desks are oaken and massive and the legislative chairs are special order, great wing-backed things that are so large that a man can sit comfortably in one and be hidden from the back. Once, when I was standing in the fishbowl, that glassed area where one can observe the legislature in action, I saw a curious sight which stayed with me. A legislator had turned his chair completely around. From my observation point and because of some optical trick, it seemed to me that he sat all alone in a sea of identically vacant chairs. Later, viewing from the other side, it seemed as if his chair was vacant and all of the others occupied.

In the morning I had a brief breakfast before I started for the legislative chambers. I had it with Ed Polsen, who's majority leader. We then walked on up. The day was cold and whistle clear. Ed, as usual, was meticulously dressed. He's one of those men of great order, able to withstand the pressure of the chaos around him. I've been in his office and marveled at his ability to live without clutter. I rather like him. He's one of those men who seem to want to involve themselves in the emotion of your life, who pick and prod at you until you've opened and bled in front of them. He told me he'd never married, but I've noticed there are always women around him. Other legislators tell admiring stories about him. He has a presence that is so powerful that it's difficult to disbelieve what he tells you.

"Thanks for picking up the slack and going to Sloan's funeral for me," he said.

"Warn't nothin', boss," I said in my best accent.

He grinned. He has the greatest of grins, completely charming. "I had to get together with some of the powers that be here—the state chairman and some of the district people. Sloan was chairman of the Judiciary Committee. It's an important job. Someone's going to have to take over for him and run that committee. It's a job with a lot of power." He looked at me directly for the first time. "How about you, Don?"

"Is that an offer?" I asked, flattered.

He grinned again and nodded. "You get first refusal. We want you as chairman."

"I'm a first-termer," I said.

He shrugged. "Inexperience may hurt you some, but you'll do okay. Putting you into the position may even reduce some of the pressure on the legislature from your college kids. That's an advantage." He nodded, as if to himself. "Advice on what needs to be done is as close as your friendly majority leader. Come see me if you have problems." He looked at me searchingly. "I'll come see you if I have any."

"You have anything in the committee?" I asked, warily interested.

He nodded. "Everyone has bills in the Judiciary." His voice moved on smoothly, without amplification: "I wouldn't want to put you under any obligation."

I smiled to myself. If he didn't want to put me under any obligation, he was using peculiar methods to accomplish that end.

All legislators constantly infight to obtain obligations. Polsen was just more competent at it than others. He reminded me of a client I'd once served, who'd owned his kind of coolness and brightness.

Ed smiled at me again and the memory faded to vagueness. . . .

"The Speaker will announce your appointment this morning," he finished.

"Who makes the appointment?" I asked. "Do you make it or does the Speaker?"

He grinned, and this time the grin was knowing and somewhat forced. "Theoretically all appointments are made by the Speaker."

I nodded, and he nodded back, and, by that time, we were at the Statehouse doors. Lobbyists were already cluttering the foyer, and we made our way into the buzzing press of them. I quickly lost Polsen to a persistent lobbyist and moved on to my locker and carefully hung my coat and hat.

Inside the chambers, busy pages flew up and down the aisles delivering messages, phone-call notes and mail. I took my seat, suddenly nervous, not really knowing why. I had a feeling that I was once again in an alien world without friend or safe hiding place. I fought it off.

Despite the fact that the hour of convening was less than five minutes away, the chambers were only about a third full. The seat on my left was empty and would remain that way. There are no methods of filling the seat of a deceased legislator in my state. Someone had already removed Sloan's little identification placard and emptied his desk drawers, leaving them slightly open. There were still a couple of pieces of mail on his desk, and I picked them up and pocketed them absently, intending to return them to the house post office so that they could be forwarded on to Sloan's executor. I ignored my own mail. There would be time for it later in the day.

The chambers began to fill, and the hierarchy made appearances. A minister prayed emotionally over us, and I'll admit we needed it badly. The day had begun.

Fat Speaker Albert McGuire stood on the raised area at the front of the chambers. Despite the fact that we're members of the same party, I don't really know him well. I sometimes have the feeling he neither likes nor approves of me, but many share this feeling in their relationship with him. He is very blunt, and his reputation is good. He'd been minority leader for years.

He leaned into his microphone and spoke in his deep, heavy voice, after the formalities were over. "As you know," he said, "we lost a member of this house quite recently. The facts surrounding his death have raised questions in the minds of many. I'm therefore forming a special committee to look into the manner of his demise and report back here to this house. I've asked Governor Bratewell to assign men from the state police to investigate this matter further and work closely with committee. To that committee I will now name the Honorable George Chapell, Edward Polsen and Donald Robak. Edward Polsen will serve as chairman." He paused and waited, looking gruffly over the microphone until the little ripple of sound subsided. "To serve in the vacancy created by the death of Sloan Link as chairman of the Judiciary Committee, I now name the Honorable Donald Robak." That brought an even greater rustle, and he smiled his cold, fatty smile and looked challengingly all around. A page brought him a note, and he looked at it. He banged his gavel, and, without announcing a reason, adjourned the house for half an hour. He retreated to his office.

I shook hands with my well-wishers and wandered down to Ed Polsen's seat. He shook my hand with great efficiency, as if he was totally surprised by what had happened.

"You didn't tell me about the special committee on Sloan Link," I said softly.

He shrugged. "What was to tell? Al's going through the motions. One of ours has been killed. We ought to know why and be informed. So he's named a committee. All you and I and George have to do is stick with the police, pick up what they come in with, and then report it back here to the house and to Al." He watched me closely. "If you want to do more, I hereby give you permission, but I'm not a policeman myself, and I'm not going to personally mix in the matter."

He watched me and then turned away, spotting George Chapell. He motioned him over.

"Inspector Robak," Chapell greeted me mockingly and shook my hand. He turned to Polsen. "Ah, Chief Inspector Polsen. A pleasure to detect with you, gentlemen. Tell me— how are things at Scotland Yard?"

Polsen gave him the grin. "I was just telling Don here that we should cool it. We let the police do their job and report that job to us. Then we report here what they give us."

Chapell nodded, and they both turned to me, waiting.

"I don't know," I said. "If he was killed because he was a member here, maybe something we know or could dredge up might help."

Chapell eyed me doubtfully. "We don't even have any definite word he was killed."

"Assuming he was killed," I said doggedly.

Polsen nodded. "I guess we can all be reasonable. We'll play it by ear. If Don here finds out, he can or *we* can be handy in this thing, assuming Link was pushed out the window, then we'll go from there."

"Okay," Chapell said grudgingly.

Polsen turned back to me. "I herewith appoint you to contact the state police working the case. See if you can be of help. Set up a line of communication with them. Tell them we must be informed of what they find. Then report everything, and I mean everything, back to Chapell and me." He nodded. "That ought to keep you from chasing that little secretary down in the attorney general's office so hard."

"What are you going to be doing while I'm doing all of this?" I asked, curious.

"I shall be sitting here, or I shall be over in the Law-lobby rooms breathlessly awaiting your report. You needn't worry about George and me. You'll be our Indian; we'll be your Chiefs."

"Ugh," Chapell said approvingly. He turned away. "How," he said over his retreating shoulder.

"My sentiments exactly," Polsen said.

The state police maintain a central office in the Statehouse up on the top floor in the old part of the building. Up there the lighting is converted gaslight fixtures, and there are areas that haven't seen any paint since World War I.

I know the top officer in the Bington District. Bington is where I maintain what is sometimes laughingly known as my "practice." He's a lieutenant, and I get impressed when I get around him because he's the only lieutenant down there, and it seems an exalted rank.

When I walked into the dim central office, the flunky who was typing reports with one finger was a lieutenant. He looked shy and diffident as he greeted me. He also looked nervous as if he was sure someone was about to take his bar away.

"My name is Donald Robak. I wanted to see whoever's in charge of the Sloan Link matter."

He nodded and poked around on his desk, frowning. Finally he found whatever it was he was looking for. He said: "That'd be Captain Carlson. He's out of the office right now." He watched me, waiting for me to say more.

"I'll wait," I said.

"Are you a newspaperman?" he asked, suspicious.

I shook my head.

He frowned and waited.

I found a chair and sat down. There was a rack of maga-

21

zines next to it. I opened one at random. The light was too bad to read.

"Where are you from?" he asked.

"Bington."

"You a lawyer?" he asked, voice now fully suspicious.

"That's right," I said.

"You represent any of those kids that are marching out there?"

"I represent them all," I said. In a way I did.

He whistled to himself softly and looked away from me. To him I represented trouble. Curiosity changed to a desire to not know much of anything.

I leafed absently through the magazine. Several times people came into the office, and I listened to the meaningless conversation. Finally the door opened, and a small, narrow man came in. He was dressed in civilian clothes. He appeared to be about fifty years old. His hair was iron gray, and there was a long, heavy scar on the left side of his face. I was sure he was an escapee from prison come to turn himself in.

"Captain Carlson," the lieutenant said, "this lawyer wants to see you." He emphasized the word lawyer. "He's from Bington," he added heavily.

Carlson turned to me, and something far back in his eyes sparked with tiny humor. "You're Robak," he said. "Glad to see you. Come on back to my office. It's a little better place to talk."

I followed him back, aware of the lieutenant watching. I was impressed that Carlson had recognized me. We went into his office. The light was better. A tiny window opened out onto a panorama of state building roofs. The walls bore signed pictures of the last four or five governors. They were smiling pictures.

He smiled also and motioned me to a seat. "I was standing back in the fishbowl behind the chambers when the Speaker named the committee," he explained. "When the break came, I saw you conferring with the other two gentlemen. I figured you got the job." His voice was soft, unaccented by regional background.

I nodded. "I'm supposed to contact you and see if I can be of help. I'm supposed to report back with whatever information seems of value. We thought that having someone from over there might also be of some value to you."

He nodded. "Okay. That seems fair enough. So far, I only know what I've read in the files given me by the Capitol City people. I haven't been up to Representative Link's room yet, although I'm going up there to take a look around." He watched me. "Want to go along?"

"Sure," I said.

"Okay, we'll go on over to the hotel in a minute." He pawed the air with a small hand. "The Capitol City boys checked Representative Link's room about a half an hour after he went out the window. It was messed up a bit. They had the hotel lock and seal it and put a policeman on watch in the next room, in case someone came back. They didn't report anything to the papers for a couple of days until they were sure no one would come back."

"He could have messed up his room himself," I said.

"They did an autopsy. He had enough booze in him when he died that the doc that did the autopsy thinks things happened after he was passed out."

"I thought there was a fight."

He shook his head. "No fight. There was noise. Stuff was scattered in hard to get at places on the floor. There was an empty bottle of Maker's Mark and another one that was open and about a third down. That's good booze, isn't it?"

I nodded. "Sippin' whiskey. Sloan liked good booze. Maker's Mark was his brand."

"There were two glasses," he said. "Both had been used.

The extra one had been smeared, so no prints. They found a lot of fingerprints on things in the room. They're checking them out." He shook his head. "I doubt that they'll do us any good. If the killer was bright enough to smear the prints on his glass, he was bright enough to do the same any other place he might have left them. Besides even finding prints wouldn't prove anything in this case. Prints wouldn't automatically mean that the person who was there was the person who shoved your Representative Link out the window." He looked over at me. "How was his capacity for liquor?"

"Just fair," I said. "He liked to drink a lot, but I've seen him pass out a couple of times. I've hauled him up to that room a time or two also."

"Someone else has seen him pass out too," he said.

I looked at his eyes and tried not to shiver. "The Speaker thinks maybe someone is bagging legislators," I said.

He nodded solemnly. "Come on," he said. "We'll go on over to the hotel."

We got up together.

Outside the weather had turned warmer. Student pickets milled near the Statehouse, calling to each other in bright and eager voices, smiling at their own homemade signs. The one I liked read: INCREASED TUITION EQUALS STUDENT COITION, and then in smaller letters, but still apparent: WE'VE BEEN SCREWED.

A couple of the students knew me and waved hello with various shades of warmth. My picture has been in the Bington *Chronicle* enough times that I'm certainly as well known as a good used-car salesman. This generation of students, at least the ones who were here fighting their battles, have learned what it's all about. I find this somewhat confusing, and my older colleagues in the house sometimes find it dismaying. The legislature normally works its session out without much glare of public interest, except that generated by the Capitol City *Enquirer's* yellow journalists in their daily hate editions. To see people around who are knowledgeable and interested is enough to shake up the veteran legislator. It didn't bother me much. They were my kids, my constituents. They hated war, and they hated useless legislation. They were in favor of anti-pollution. They had an opinion on most everything. They'd helped elect me by going door to door, by working the polls for me. I owed them.

Some of the older legislators seem to believe there is something suspicious about involvement. That isn't my feeling. Sometimes I think the young ones are only biding their time until they have a clear majority. The world may then be a startling place.

It may even be a saner place.

It was a good thing that I was fated to be a one-termer. Lots of people thought that. Maybe even the wilder of the students.

Captain Carlson was watching me covertly.

"I swear I don't know where they've got the dynamite and LSD hid out," I said.

He didn't smile. "Some of those people there are the ones who do have the dynamite and the LSD and the hard narcotics."

I shook my head. "No, Captain. There are several little groups of students up here. Those that you see out there walking in the bright light of day are the kids who are trying to save things. If a riot started, some of those kids might throw stones, might break windows. That's all. But there's another group, a group that uses those people there, preys on them. Some of those kids marching there know the angry ones, know what they're doing. But the only involvement they have is the act of knowing. They don't want your buildings blown up any more than you want them blown up. But between you and those others, there isn't a real choice for them." I looked back at the marchers. "Most of those there will take anything that happens that, for example, reduces tuition, as a victory. But the ones who hide out during the day and only come out after dark won't be satisfied with anything. If you gave them this state, they'd want the country. They don't know what they want—they only know that it isn't whatever you give them. The only ones who can control them are those kids with the signs."

He grinned. "A philosopher," he said.

"Don't laugh," I said softly. "What I'm talking about is the beginning and also maybe the end."

"It was the war," he said.

"Partly," I agreed.

He sighed, and we proceeded.

Sloan Link's room was not only locked, it was also padlocked. The captain unlocked the locks carefully, and we entered. Dust had seeped in from an open, screened window and it hung in the air, blurring the sunshine.

"All those papers over there on the table were around on the floor. Most of them had been picked up and put in a stack, but there were some under the bed and some others around in places where someone in a hurry might not have noticed them. It looked like someone had thrown them all over and then picked them up later."

I looked at the papers. They were copies of legislative measures that had been introduced. The stack was respectable, probably a foot high, which I estimated would pretty well take care of what we'd had so far.

"It might be nice to know what's in that stack and what isn't in it," I said.

26

He nodded. "We beat you to it. The Capitol City detectives ran the list and checked what was here against what had been introduced. I've a copy of the list of the missing bills over in the office. I'll send you the list."

"Thanks." I looked around the room nervously. To be in the room seemed a violation of some shadowy someone's privacy. "You say the doctor said he was passed out. Maybe he woke up or maybe he never passed out. Drunks are funny. He could have gone through the window himself."

Captain Carlson smiled gently. "There are some other things. There's a very good possibility that he was dead before he went out the window. I didn't tell you that before. The official story is that he either jumped or was pushed, and we're leaning toward the idea he was pushed. That's what was in all of the papers. But he hit on a car roof when he landed down below. He hit so that his back and shoulders caught the car roof, and his head hit nothing. The snap of hitting broke his neck, but it didn't injure his head." He looked up at me. "But there were head injuries. Someone had taken a pipe or some heavy piece of material and used it on his head causing massive injuries. I think they then pushed him out the window to disguise what had happened."

"Maybe he hit something going down?" I asked.

He shook his head. "It's a possibility. We didn't find anything showing he hit going down." He shrugged. "It's also possible that he hit headfirst into the car roof and then slid forward, but the injuries weren't right, Representative Robak."

"Call me Don," I said.

He hesitated. "All right," he said finally.

"Why the mystery?" I asked. "Why not give out the word to the papers about what you theorize happened?"

He looked at me wearily. "You get nuts. We've had three

27

of them so far who confessed to the murder. All three are pretty well-known nuts. They confess to most murders that happen around this town that get much publicity. So the local police and our people are pretty careful about what they turn loose in the way of actual information." He looked at me narrowly. "And there's another thing I want you to think about."

"What's that?"

"There isn't any certainty that this is the only murder there's going to be. If the killer is a psycho, it's possible that he will kill again, like your Speaker McGuire said. If the legislature is his target, then all of your people should be warned. But we don't have enough yet to do that, and I don't want to start a panic." He said it all slowly, as if he was musing to himself, going over it again and trying to discover some flaw in the reasoning process.

"I can't really believe that," I said.

He smiled without humor. "You were telling me about those kids out there. If they'll blow up buildings, then they'll kill. Maybe we've got a conspiracy going on. Link was carrying a tuition-raise bill, and that's the focal point of all of the protest. So maybe they murdered him."

"Right now it's maybe a million times," I said.

"You ever been involved in a murder case?"

I nodded.

He nodded back, considering me. "I suspect I'd better check on you," he said.

"Sure. Can I look around a little more?" I asked.

"Go ahead," he said. He went to the window and took the chair nearby, sitting so that he could gaze out and down at the student marchers.

I looked around. Nothing seemed to be out of order except that the mirror on the bureau was cracked. I went into the bathroom and opened the medicine closet. Sloan's shaving gear was still there. Nothing seemed out of the way.

The room was just another hotel room in an old hotel. It was about like mine.

I went back out and up to the captain. "Could you have someone shoot me copies of what you got from the Capitol City police and send it over to me?"

He nodded carefully.

"Thanks," I said. "Thank you also for showing me the room."

He nodded again, and I left him sitting in the chair, still watching the marchers below with eyes that didn't quite believe what they saw.

I went back to the Statehouse and carefully skirted the line of marchers and went up to my office on the third floor. I would want to talk to some of the kids, but that could wait till later, till questions had crystallized. I sat there for a while thinking, but nothing useful came. It was midafternoon. I left my office and went down marble stairs worn by the traffic of the years to the attorney general's office. The receptionist nodded to me, and I slipped past her and on back to the office where Judy worked.

She was beating a fair rhythm on her electric typewriter, lips pursed in concentration. She had her hair drawn back and tied with a bright ribbon, and she looked all of seventeen.

"Coffee?" I asked.

She frowned. "I'm way behind. I'll never catch up." She looked at me and then smiled. "However, it's the best offer I've had in the last fifteen minutes. I'll go quietly."

We went down another flight of steps into the basement of the building. In the far corner they've built a little coffee shop. I ordered black coffee, and she ordered tea.

"I wanted to tell you that I wouldn't be around tonight," I said.

"Oh," she said with minor frost.

"I got appointed to a committee that's looking into Sloan's death. I thought I'd try to find out where he was before, on the night someone pushed him out the window."

"I could go along," she said in a small voice.

"It may not be very interesting. I'm just going to go places and ask irritating questions." I brightened remembering that where Sloan had passed there were usually bright lights and good whiskey. "I suppose we could get some dinner along the way and I would like having you along."

"I don't want to be a bother," she said, mollified.

"A bother you aren't."

And so it was agreed and I took her back to her office and then wandered back into legislative territory.

I found that I was suddenly immensely more popular with lobbyists than I'd been. Gentlemen of the corridors who'd previously ignored me suddenly had extra large smiles for me, knew my name, mangled my hand with congratulations.

I spent the afternoon in session. We passed a couple of bills. One of them turned a small part of a state park over to a city that needed the land for a dual-lane highway. The other one wasn't *that* important. I yawned until break time. I voted against the park giveaway. I figured the people who used the park needed it as much as the city needed the highway expansion, which was an obstructionist point of view.

Afterward there were some committee meetings. Banks Committee, of which I was a member, had one. I went there and let them use me to make a quorum. Then I left and went to the house secretary's office. I asked them in there to make me a list of all bills now in the Judiciary Committee. They promised it to me for the morrow.

CHAPTER III

RULE 6. *Lobbyists, properly licensed and registered, shall be allowed to appear before legislative committees to give testimony and impart information.*

At six that evening, somewhat sanitary after a lingering, singing shower, I presented myself at the Law-lobby rooms. I had the inevitable drink shoved into my protesting but outstretched hand and awaited Judy St. Avery. She'd agreed to meet me there.

The party was going hard. In addition to the normal noise there was something new. In a far corner a group of sheriffs had set up an amateur barbershop quartet. They were "Mill Streaming" and "Workin' On the Railroad" in total concentration, ignoring all other sounds. I wandered over and listened, found they didn't need a tenor, and wandered farther. Besides, I was sung out from the shower.

A large drunk I didn't know came up and put a restraining arm around my shoulders.

"You're Robak, ain't you?" he asked with that tone in his voice that signifies half belligerence, half alcohol.

"Sure," I said.

He looked me over carefully. "No," he said. "You're not Robak. I've seen Robak." He loosed my shoulders disappointedly. "You're not him."

I nodded agreeably and spotted Judy at the door. I moved away while he was still eying me doubtfully.

"Robak's a bastard," he said resentfully to my back and I grinned and went on.

"Hi," she said. She was dressed modestly in green and all she did to me was temporarily stop my heart. I saw other men eying her and I, possession proud, took her small, gloved hand.

"Hello to you," I said softly.

"Where are we going first?" she asked.

I thought about it. "No sense asking here. He never came around this place. He'd had some sort of falling out with his sheriff and he just refused to come here." I looked down at her and tried to remember about Sloan Link. It was difficult. "Once I had to meet Sloan over here in the hotel," I mused. "I think I met him up at the Financial-lobby rooms. He hung out there sometimes. At least it would be somewhere to start. They've got the hotel penthouse."

We went on out of the Law rooms. Behind us the party continued unabated. The hotel corridor that we walked needed paint and the carpet was beginning to wear in the center. The hall smelled of disinfectant and departed tenants.

"They're going to tear it down," she said, sensing my inspection.

"What?"

"This hotel. I hear they're going to put up another parking garage. There was a story in the paper. Didn't you read it?"

I smiled. "I seldom read the paper, Judy. My party calls it the *Ex-Lax Express* and your party doesn't object when we do it. I guess I don't read it because I don't want to know why they call it that."

We caught the elevator and perilously rode up seven more floors to the penthouse.

The Financial-lobby rooms seemed different from the rooms that Law maintained. There was a bar, but nobody made an issue out of shoving a drink into our hands. There were people there, but the crowd was soberer, sparser and quieter. A smartly uniformed bartender hovered obsequiously behind the bar. His wise eyes surveyed me, recognized me.

"Would you care for a drink, Representative Robak?"

I ordered for Judy and myself and he began making the drinks with adroit hands.

In a far corner men of commerce saw me, tinkled glasses wisely, and murmured among themselves. One finally detached himself from the crowd and came languidly over.

"Nice to see you, Representative Robak," he said easily. He tried to make his voice blend with the stereo that played softly in the background. I craned to hear and recognize the tune. "I'm William Jucker." He smiled a charming smile and I tried to estimate his age, deciding that he could be anything from a dissipated thirty to a well-preserved fifty. "You might say I'm your host," he continued. "I'm with the Capitol City First National." He reached out for my hand and I gave it to him and he massaged it gently and waited.

"This is Judy St. Avery," I said.

He nodded and looked appreciative.

"Why I'm here," I said slowly, feeling a hunch, "is that I got appointed to a committee to look into the death of Sloan Link. The committee had a report that he was up here on the night he was killed," I lied. "Who was he with and what was he doing?"

He frowned slightly. "I think he was here for a few moments early that evening. I don't recall that he was with anyone. I suppose he came in, as he often did, had a drink or two, and then left." He nodded as if what he'd said explained it all. "Of course we were shocked to hear of his death."

"Did he leave with anyone?"

"I don't know," he said and looked over at the bartender. "Frank?" he queried.

The bartender shrugged. "I don't remember," he said.

I nodded speculatively at the bartender, not sure whether he was telling the truth. "I'd appreciate it if you'd ask around, Frank." I turned back to Jucker. "Anything you can do to help us will be appreciated by the committee."

Jucker nodded vaguely. "Of course we're happy to be of help."

I cracked the whip a little. "If things don't go well for us I suppose we'll have to call witnesses to appear in front of the committee. I'd certainly hate to do that with people in sensitive positions."

He blanched. I could see him reading future headlines: "BANK EXECUTIVE CALLED IN MURDER INVESTIGATION."

I turned to Judy to give him time to think about the situation.

"The view is really something from up here," I said. "I want you to see it."

She nodded and we walked away leaving Jucker. Out of the corner of my eye I saw him turn to Frank the bartender and they fell into a low-voiced conversation.

The night outside was whistle clear. You could see most of Capitol City. To the south there was a park. It looked like a nice park, although the trees were now winter bare. Today the Capitol City delegation had voted en masse for the highway across a neighboring city's park. I wondered how much they'd scream if someone tried to build a highway across their park?

Judy took my hand. "It doesn't look like snow," she said. "The weather forecaster said snow."

We turned away from the window. There was a fireplace in the near corner of the room. I thought about the fact that I was chasing after a murderer and I was suddenly cold. I eased toward the fire and then saw the grate contained only an electric log.

Jucker, the bank man, nodded at me from the bar. It was evident from his expression that he wanted to tell me something. I took Judy's hand and walked over.

"Frank thinks he remembers something that might be of help," Jucker said unctuously. "I'll let him tell you."

"Thanks," I said.

I went on to the bar.

The bartender's face was cautiously friendly. He leaned toward me. "They told me, when I got this job, to forget what I saw and heard here, Representative Robak. So I never say anything about what I hear or see." He shook his head. "Now they change around and tell me to remember." He shrugged. "So I remember. I guess it was the night he was killed. The nights here are pretty much the same, but it was the last night Representative Link was around. He had a couple of drinks and then he left with Mr. Toy."

"T. J. Toy?" I asked.

"I don't know his full name," he said. "He's a sort of heavy fellow who's a lobbyist. Comes here now and then. Wears nice clothes."

"Thank you, Frank," I said. "Anything else?"

"No, sir," he said, voice positive, and I believed him. "I never saw Mr. Link again, but Mr. Toy's been in once or twice since that night."

"You don't remember them saying where they were going?"

He shook his head. "No, sir. Mr. Link had an argument with someone that night, but I can't remember who it was now." He nodded at Jucker. "I asked him, but he doesn't remember either."

"He had an argument here?" I asked, feeling excitement rise within me.

"I think it was that night. Some political thing."

I nodded. And then Sloan wound up dead. I had a place to go now. T. J. Toy. I knew T. J. Toy fairly well. He'd taken me out one night and given me his guided tour of Capitol City. It had included most of the places that boys are supposed to like, i.e., to wit: The topless houses and the semi-strip joints. There'd also been a second-rate meal at a steakhouse ill-famed among the legislators for such meals. That night and the almost inedible steak would have been bearable but for one thing: T. J. Toy.

There's a sort of unwritten code among lobbyists. A lobbyist can be bleeding and dying for a bill or up in arms against another, but he will never, I repeat, *never*, push at you when you're on the town with him.

T. J. Toy had pushed. He'd not only pushed, he'd entreated and cajoled. He'd done about everything except ask me how much I'd take to vote against anti-pollution. I'd laughed him off, refused to take him seriously, and refused all offers to tour the town with him thereafter.

T.J. was a mean-eyed fat man who wore really great clothes. He was without distinction otherwise and so people, like the bartender, wound up remembering the clothes. I'd even heard one legislator say that his employers should just send the clothes to the legislative corridors and leave T.J. at home.

This session T.J. was pimping hard for an outfit known as the Air of Liberty lobby. The name was impressive, but the purpose was only devious. It was a lobby set up by a shadowy group of manufacturers, utilities and industries to supposedly protect themselves from harsh anti-pollution controls.

T.J. was the front, the paid lobbyist. I doubted that he was a part of the brain trust.

Lobbyists are normally useful to legislators. They furnish needed information and convey what certain groups want to legislators. Most lobbyists are impeccably honest and their word is accepted as true without question or comment.

And then there was T.J. I'd heard there was a lot of money around and available through the lobby. I'd heard that some of the boys had taken advantage of it and really got lush treatment. Many of them, of course, were only playing old T.J. along for nights on the town and overfriendly dancing girls and maybe a few of the other good things that a legislative session can hold. I'd heard that others had gone further.

I guess he'd bought me a second-rate meal because I was a first-timer just in from the hinterlands. I guess he'd tried hard with me, violated his lobbyist's code, because he figured I'd never know any better. And I wondered what he was thinking now. Anti-pollution was in *my* committee. I was the man sitting on T. J. Toy's spout.

I turned to Judy and took her arm. "Let's find a cab and go look for Mr. Toy."

We found him at Jeanine's. That's a place out in an area of the city known as the Sex Strip. Jeanine's is typical for that section. It has a dirty, mock-colonial front with huge signs showing dancing girls and bubbling cocktails. That's what they serve. Inside the main attraction is a big piano that takes up about half of the space. It has booths and seats around it. I guess most of the piano's insides are merely bracing because on the top of the piano dancing girls go-go frenetically. They wear costumes that most gentlemen find at least sparsely interesting.

T.J. had a ringside seat. A couple of legislators I knew were sitting self-consciously near him. Four girls were dancing on the piano top. The largest thing they were wearing was that professional, put-on smile which is sad in its attempt to convey gaiety. They were dancing close to where the legislators were and the hour was late enough. I figured this might be the place where T.J.'s golden promises of a big, big evening would pay off. Maybe later my two legislative compatriots could writhe about in unenthusiastic, competent, paid-for sin. Now, they eyed me and wondered who I'd tell about seeing them with T.J.

Judy held my hand tightly. This was the fourth place we'd searched following the trail of T. J. Toy. The first two had been fairly tame (or between shows), but in the third a nearly naked woman had greeted us at the door, eyed Judy's modest dress, then boldly opened the two top buttons.

"Get comfortable, doll," she'd said to Judy, who'd blushed. Gamely, Judy had gone on with me even though her heart wasn't in it. Things were a little frigid still because I'd laughed. Now she seemed prepared to flee at the drop of a stripper's G string.

We went on back to the piano bar. The seats were crowded and T.J. and his friends hadn't seen us yet. I tapped T.J. on the shoulder.

"Robak!" he exclaimed, his voice only slightly thick. He inspected Judy with care. "No wonder I couldn't interest you in a night on the town." He nodded. "I like a man who rolls his own," he said with unimpeachable vulgarity.

"I need to talk to you," I said.

"Here?" he questioned. "Now?"

I nodded.

I could almost see things ticking over his head. I wasn't drunk; I had my own girl; he'd already offered money. He eyed me with suspicion. Then he remembered that I had his bill in my committee.

He nodded. "Sit here, honey," he said to Judy and got up.

I squeezed her hand. "I'll only be a moment or two," I said apologetically.

I tapped the nearest legislator. "Watch her," I said. "Take care of her."

"Just as if she was my own," he said, grinning evilly.

We walked on back to the men's room. Inside an attendant was putting ice in the urinal. He watched us from afar suspiciously, for deviational behavior. His eyes were as old as the centuries.

"You were out with Sloan Link the night he died," I said to T.J.

He recoiled a little. "Not me, friend," he demurred. "You've got the wrong man."

"I hear otherwise."

He shrugged carefully. "I can't help what you hear." He waited for a moment and then smiled a restless smile. "I've got those people out there. I'd better get back. Why don't you and your little doll join us for an evening on the town —though this is about the end of it."

I didn't move. "You were seen, T.J."

His face reddened a little, but the fixed smile didn't waver. "I'll tell you again that you're wrong. Your informants are mistaken."

I smiled back at him. "All right, mister. You say you weren't, other people say you were. I guess the only thing to do is call you as a witness before the committee."

"Up to you," he said, unshaken.

"And one more thing," I said. "Tomorrow the Judiciary Committee meets. I'm going to put the pressure on to report out the anti-pollution bill with a recommendation for passage without amendment. And it's tough the way it is. Then I'm going to hold every possible bill in that committee and also hold every senate bill that gets referred there until anti-pollution is passed. Meantime I'm going to spread the word that you're why I'm doing it, so it gets back to your bosses."

He watched me. For the first time there was something other than alcohol and boredom in his eyes. "Why are you doing this?" he asked, voice deadly.

"Sloan Link was a friend," I said. "I want to know what happened to him. I've got witnesses who put you with him on the night he was killed. I want to know where you went, what you did, who you saw, and who can verify it. If you lie to me about anything and I find it out I swear I'll drop anti-pollution out of my committee recommended 'do-pass' and use it to shut off your lights and traveling money. I'm for the bill now, with some reservations. If you tell me the truth then I'll just treat it in the normal manner." I watched him. "Up to you."

"I've got some connections that can stop it—stop you," he flared.

"Use them," I said laconically. "Everyone's got bills in the Judiciary. I find anyone moving around tough trying to stop me then any bill they want will stay right there under my thumb in that committee."

He looked at me and knew I could do it. A chairman has a

great deal of that kind of power. He pulled his handkerchief and dabbed at his forehead and resolve crumbled.

"I was only with him for a while," he said. "I didn't know he was going out that window later." He eyed me sourly. "Who told you I was with him?"

I shook my head. "Just tell me what you did and who you saw. I'll use what I already know to check your story."

"I met him up at the Financial room, the one in the Blue Hotel penthouse. We had a couple of drinks there. We left when his old flame came in."

"Who's that?" I asked. To the best of my knowledge Link hadn't had a serious girl.

"Gertrude May. She's the one that's secretary of the senate. I guess they've been feuding most of this session. At least when she came in he wanted to go." He snapped his fingers. "I forgot something. He had an argument there with McGuire, the Speaker. They were at it when I came into the penthouse rooms. I thought McGuire was going to try him. They were both pretty mad." He shrugged. "A few minutes later they were back grinning at each other. When we left, Link told McGuire he'd see him later and they shook hands." He shook his head. "Politicians! I'll never understand them."

"What were they arguing about?" I asked, interested.

"I don't know," he said. He watched my face. "I'm not kidding you or trying to hold something from you. I just don't know. I even asked around about it, after Link died. No one seemed to know what they were arguing about. It just flared up all of a sudden." He hesitated. "Maybe it was something political. I've heard that Speaker McGuire wants to run for the U. S. Senate and that Link wasn't supporting him. I've also heard they just never did get along."

"Where'd you go when you left the Blue?" I asked.

"Out on the town. We hit a few bars. I had a sweet little lady I was going to fix him with, but he got sort of drunk." He laughed without humor. "In fact, both of us got drunk. I finally hauled him back to the hotel and left him there before midnight. I never saw him again. Next day I heard he'd gone out the window." He shook his head. "I didn't want to get in trouble."

"Who else did you see while you were out that night?"

He thought hard about it. Finally he shook his head. "It got pretty drunk out. I remember the early part of the evening okay, but the later part is sort of fuzzy. I remember we talked to some people, but then Link was always talking to people. I can tell you where we went if that would help. Maybe you could check it out. I do remember buying drinks for some other legislators." He tapped his forehead. "Then there was some kind of agent or something that sat with us for a while. Link maybe knew him. I guess he was an insurance agent. I think I can tell you where we went if that would help."

"Who were the legislators?"

He shook his head irritably. "I spend my days and nights talking with legislators. I can't separate one legislator from another." He looked at me bleakly. "I'll tell you where we went. Maybe you can dig out something you need by checking those places."

I nodded. "Okay, T.J."

"We started at Tansey's. That's the fish place down near the interstate. Link was fond of it. After we ate we went to George's Rendezvous. That's a black-and-tan place." He nodded to himself. "I think that's where the other legislators were. Link was talking to them and I bought them all drinks. Then we went on to Big Bad Al's. That's a topless joint. I had a cute girl in there wanted to see him. That's where this guy came over and sat with us. I don't know who he was, but the waitress introduced him to me." He gave me a hopeless look. "As far as that's concerned, we sat in there with a whole big bunch of people at a table. Al's was crowded. So we sat with these people. Link knew them. I got shuffled down to the end of the table. That's where this agent guy was. Link and he were talking and Link was pretty drunk. So, in a little while, we left and went back to the Blue and I dropped him there. I went on out to my place."

"Where do you live, T.J.?"

"At the Athletic Club. I'm staying there through the session." He smiled. "One of my sponsors arranged it."

"How'd Link stand on anti-pollution?"

"He was pushing it. I was trying the best I could to get him to hold it up, maybe amend it to death. But we didn't talk about that during that last night." He smiled stiffly. "Lobbyists don't mix business with pleasure."

I smiled also. I guess he'd conveniently forgotten our voyage night. He'd been a little drunk that night. And he'd been pushy with me. I wondered how pushy he'd gotten with Link? I wondered also if this fat little man could have killed Link? Link was pushing anti-pollution. T. J. Toy was fighting it. With all his heart, soul and someone else's well-filled billfold.

"Who's really back of your little lobby group, T.J.?"

"A lot of worried people," he said guardedly. "No one particular person. But I *will* tell you that some of those worried people are from your county, Robak."

"Sure," I said easily. "Sure they are." I watched him. "Keep on spreading the cheer for them, T.J. Keep the cute ladies available and the whiskey flowing and buy yourself a lot of votes. Just maybe you'll wind up, by reaction, with what you don't want shoved into you by a fat vote."

43

"A Christer," he said, eyes shrewd. "I'll bet you're just too good to do anything wrong, Robak." He smiled. "What do you do with that little lady out there—hold hands?"

I smiled, but I was stung a little. "Maybe. What we do is our own affair and none of yours. I'm talking about the legislature."

He shook his head. "We'll take our chances. I told you what you wanted. Now you play it fair like you said you would."

I nodded.

"And talk to me before you do anything foolish," he added, back to being a lobbyist again.

We left, to the relief of the attendant.

CHAPTER IV

RULE 9. *Committees shall act upon all bills as soon as is prudently practicable.*

I dropped Judy at her apartment after complimenting her for being a brave, adventurous girl. I was rewarded with an extra long, not completely chaste good-night kiss. That kiss partly removed the residual sting of T.J.'s taunt. I went on back to the hotel in good spirits. Outside a fine mist of snow was falling, turning dirty sidewalks clean, collecting on car windows. The wind was cold. Near the hotel two old alcoholics huddled in an alcove, splitting a bottle against the bitter night. They regarded my stare carefully and hid the bottle a little. Maybe I looked like I needed a drink out of their lives. I heard them laugh hollowly after I'd passed.

I went to my room and double-locked the door. A *precaution.*

And then I couldn't sleep. I kept remembering Sloan Link and what he'd been like. For I'd been out with him the night before the night that T.J. had tried to describe. We'd had many drinks, but I guess it's that I'm younger than T.J. I remembered all of that night. The alcohol didn't block my memory.

We'd gone to Gaillo's, which purports to be an Italian place, but doesn't make it. They served us bad spaghetti and slightly better wine. Jim Rucknall, a railroad lobbyist, had taken us.

I remember Link sprawled at the table. He was an enormous man with hands that were huge, a long, clownish face, and sparse, fading hair. There was something magnetic about him. He knew people everywhere, never forgot their names. And, of course, they knew him. He was generous to his friends, vicious to his enemies. I'd heard it said of him that when he wanted he could charm the pants off a twenty-year-old virgin, if such a thing still exists. I've also heard him described as perhaps the only man who could have started a fight at Christ's last supper. He was so vital that it made men and women feel immortal when they were near him.

He'd been drunk and I'd been drinking. Jim Rucknall had been called to the phone to talk to someone about a merger. Gaillo's place smelled of garlic and stale beer.

Link was in an expansive mood.

"You're coming along, Robak," he said. "I think you're going to be one of the good ones, the ones who last. I think you'll spend a lot of years here in the legislature."

I grinned. "No, Sloan. It isn't going to be that way. Where I come from I'm lucky to be here this once. It won't ever happen again."

He shrugged. "Well, do the best you can for yourself this time. Make some connections."

"You instructed me about that before too," I joked. "I can follow directions. I left the transom to my hotel room open last night like you said. You know, so they could throw the bags of money over. All I found this morning was a slightly used prophylactic and an empty wine bottle."

He laughed. "A fellow has to be patient. You'll get there."

He leaned toward me and the laughter left his face. "Just don't get so sharp you cut your own throat, Don." He smiled hauntingly. "Some do. Even I do at times."

"What's the problem, Sloan?" I asked.

He smiled again and tapped the table with enormous knuckles. "Too many years on good and bad booze, too many times to the well. Nothing to show for it. My bones are cold." He looked over at me slyly. "You see before you the remnants of a once vigorous man."

"Come off it," I said. "I know you too well. You've got a play for every occasion. What tragedy is it tonight?"

He grinned hugely. "Representative Lear, maybe. But you really don't know me that well, Don. Only about a month."

"You get to know people pretty quickly up here," I said.

He nodded agreeably. "It is a little world of its own." He looked away and grew pensive again. "We fight out our battles and play our intrigues with one another, insert the knife, then withdraw. And somehow each of us views the whole overall thing as a holy grail where the end justifies the means." He nodded. "I guess that's the way it is."

I looked him over. If we weren't good friends then he was at least the best acquaintance I'd ever made. He'd helped me in the legislature, been available to me, counseled me. His mind was a well-oiled computer that was stuffed full of legislative lore. He'd forgotten more than most legislators would ever know, but he was without real arrogance about it.

And he drank far too much.

Someone had shaped the clown face with a crazed hatchet, then dropped two questing, blue eyes in the proper spots. Those eyes had seen it all, catalogued it, and laughed all of the time the observation was taking place. The neck and body below were oversized, the feet and hands gargantuan.

47

The clothes were merely covering, not bought for style. He told me that, in sessions past, he'd always made the list of the ten worst-dressed legislators, as chosen by the news media.

Another legislative lawyer once pompously told me that lawyers made the best legislators. Sloan Link was the exception that proved the rule. He ran a down-at-the-heels lumberyard in a tiny northern town. Business had been bad, so he'd gotten into politics. He'd run and won the nomination and then the election for the assembly. That first time had been a fight. Since then no one had even come close, although they yapped after him each election.

He was a man of small education, but much native shrewdness. He had committed the rules of the house to memory and could roll them off at request. His I.Q. was probably off the top end of the scale.

I'd heard others say that he could have been governor, or at least had the nomination of my party for governor. He'd never attempted to get that nomination and discouraged friends who tried to push him. He told me: "I don't want to be governor. A governor has power for four years and then he's a dead pigeon. I've been running this state for a lot longer than that and those guys who sit down there in the governor's office still think they're running it." He shook his head. "The damned fools." Then, as always, the huge, infectious laugh.

He'd been a good friend. I'd liked him very much, admired him even more. Now he was dead and there was anger in me about the way he'd died.

There had to be a *why*. I wondered what that *why* had been. And I wondered about T. J. Toy.

You can hear stories about every legislator who's been

around for some years. Stories about money. Everyone has his suspectors. When Sloan had been alive I'd heard stories about him. I hadn't believed them.

Now he was dead.

I still didn't believe them, but now they had to be taken into the reckoning.

Sloan had always kidded about taking money, joked about how much was available. Yet he'd seemed to steer away from those who were openly on the take.

Legislators joke about the take. It's their best joke, but it's a nervous sort of thing. Always there's the wondering about what price a friend has.

So far they hadn't found mine. I wondered if they'd found Link's.

Link had been a good legislator. He respected the pecking order. The orders on things that were part of politics came from the party hierarchy. Sloan followed them.

And he was respected because his word was good. He was respected because he stayed in the rules and knew them better than anyone else.

But he was poor. There wasn't any money base for Sloan, no fat tree to pick for good apples.

He told me that night: "I'm old and cold, Don. I'll be sixty-one my next birthday. I want—"

I'd waited but he'd never finished.

We'd managed to get drunker. We went from the Italian place on out to Fresno Bob's, which is an old-fashioned bar with peanuts on the tables. You're supposed to shell them and throw the husks on the sawdust floor.

Sloan had known almost everyone in Bob's. That night he'd been a happy man. Certainly there was no intention to throw himself out a window. So he'd been pushed or thrown.

And someone had coldly done it. I didn't even like thinking about who the killer could be, unless it could be T.J. or one of his hirelings.

That might be it.

I went to sleep sitting there in my one comfortable chair in the hotel room.

Once I came awake and I thought what had wakened me was someone in the hall outside my room. For a long time I sat there, unmoving, listening.

Nothing happened.

I got up finally and went to bed.

In my dreams a nightmare tamperer at my door made it in. I couldn't see his/her face, but I was quickly found in my hiding place.

And then, with a bloody ax, he/she . . .

In the morning I was unimpressed with the nightmare. I had other problems to worry with. I regarded myself in the mirror on the door of my bathroom and decided I was getting fat. High living was doing it to me. I was having martinis for lunch at the Press Club, followed by chili and a cheeseburger. I was having free coffee and doughnuts in the legislative caucus rooms after breakfast. And at night I was being wined and dined by some lobbyist, or Judy was feeding me like a harvest hand at her table.

I did a few deep knee bends, but my heart wasn't in it. I was fat, but I wasn't *that* fat yet. I resolved that I'd go up to the Athletic Club and have a swim, some handball, and a steam bath this very day. Then I'd do it every day. And I'd walk. I'd stop taking cabs when I had to go someplace within reasonable walking distance.

Fortified by that resolve I decided to go out and have a huge breakfast to celebrate my determination. So I rode the elevator down. Outside there was only a little snow on the ground and the day was very cold. The wind was from the northwest and you could smell meat-packing houses in it. Sirens were already screaming in the distance. The traffic was fierce. Another day had begun in the city and I was glad I was from Bington, glad I'd be going back there to face only college protests and riots in a few more weeks. I didn't like the city.

I walked on up to my favorite breakfast place and spied Fred Olean in a far corner and joined him.

"You appear to have slept well," he commented.

"The sleep of the innocent," I said. "Judy and I eveninged out and did some tracking on Sloan Link's final night. Found out some places he'd been." I watched him quizzically. "You know anything about a place called George's Rendezvous?"

He nodded. "I know George Herbert. He owns it."

"Sloan was there that night. There maybe were some other legislators around. T. J. Toy was picking up the tab. T.J. says he was stoned enough that he doesn't remember who was there or what went on. Would there be anyone around the place up there who could or would tell me?"

"George himself, maybe," he said slowly. "He's kind of an *aficionado* of the political process. Collects people. Maybe he thinks people like you and me can fix things for him if he gets in trouble. If he was there then he'd know what went on. He's a big gent and he runs that place all the way."

"Would he tell me?" I asked.

"I guess he would if I was along." He grinned at me. "That's what you were angling for, wasn't it?"

"You bet." I reached out and got his breakfast check. "Just for that, boy," I said in my best overbearing manner, "I'm going to fix this ticket for you." I nodded and changed faces.

51

"You can treat me like any other lobbyist, but don't kiss at my hands."

"Thank you so much, Massa Bossie," he said solemnly. "Oh, when the revolution come I'm goin' to hide you out. For a while. . . ." He leaned forward conspiratorially. "Now, I want to know the real reason you're buying my breakfast. What do you want me to vote for or against today."

I came to mock attention. "For God and the flag and some legal types of motherhood. And I'll ask you to vote against sin. That should do it."

He nodded and something about his solemnity broke me up and in a moment we were both bent double, scandalizing several waitresses of different colors but with bigoted leanings.

I picked up my list of bills in the Judiciary Committee from the secretary of the house. It was an imposing list. There were more than seventy bills languishing in the committee. I went out to the big blackboard and chalked on a notice that Judiciary would meet on adjournment that afternoon. I noted further that we'd consider all bills.

I put down the chalk and stood back to examine my notice. Several lobbyists watched me. One of them was T. J. Toy. He nodded; Ed Polsen came up beside me and checked the notice over also.

"You ought to put down a time," he said.

"Just 'On Adjournment,'" I said. "If I put down a time then maybe we'll run past that time in session today."

He shrugged. "You really going to try to consider all bills?"

"Well, anything anyone wants. There are more than seventy bills hung up. Some of them probably should be on the floor for action. Some of them ought to be dead. A lot of them are going to require study, maybe even hearings. I need to know which is which."

"The minutes of previous hearings should help," he said considerately. "Might let you cut out worrying with some that have already been weeded out."

"Good idea," I said. "I've missed some of the committee meetings because I had to make other meetings. Can you get me copies of the minutes of the other meetings?"

"Sure," he said. "Anyone could get them. The gal that takes them is supposed to type them up after every meeting. I'll have her run enough copies so that all of the committee members can have them." He shook his head and eyed me with minor condescension. "Link never used notes. He had a fabulous memory."

"I'm not that well off." I looked at him. "You liked Link, didn't you, Ed?"

"He was the best they ever made. Anything new on it?"

I considered Ed, liking him. If his opinion of Link had been good, then Link's opinion of Ed had exceeded it. Once I heard Link refer to him as the brightest, sharpest legislator this side of California. "Chapell," he said, "is crude compared to Ed. Chapell grouses here and there, threatens his way into deals, but in the meantime Ed's cut nine throats while Chapell is whetting his knife. And always with a smile. You have to watch Chapell. He and McGuire act on instinct. Polsen thinks. Chapell is dangerous when he's angry, but recovers quickly."

I came back to present time and present places. Link was dead.

I snapped my fingers. "I wanted to tell Chapell and you that I found out some places Sloan had been before he went out the window. I did some checking last night and am going to do some more tonight. I've got him covered up to midnight now as to where he was."

He stepped back from me and looked me over as if he was

really seeing me for the first time. "You're really serious about all of this, aren't you? You truly think you can do more than the police?"

I shook my head. "No. Absolutely not. But maybe I can get some information that will help the police."

He nodded. "That would be great," he said, smiling. "Chapell and I talked yesterday when you weren't around. We don't want any boat rocking going on, no inquisition. We don't want anything that could hurt the legislature."

"Friend," I said softly, "we're already in a hurtful situation. One of our own has been killed. The newspapers up and down the state have trumpeted it, the radio and television howled it. People out there are wondering what's going on. Maybe we can help find out. I think we *need* to find out."

He nodded. "Okay, okay," he soothed. "I agree. Just be extra careful."

I nodded back.

"How about some coffee and doughnuts?" he asked.

"You, sir, are the fat and gentle voice of temptation," I said. I followed him on to the caucus room where legislators were dunking doughnuts and the conversation was running free. Suffering a hurtful conscience, I held myself to a lone doughnut.

There I heard that the house leaders were in conference deciding some weighty issue and that we wouldn't convene for probably another hour or so. Polsen left to attend.

CHAPTER V

RULE 11. *The house of representatives and the senate are empowered to employ such persons as are necessary to assist in operating and maintaining each house.*

It seemed a fitting time to check out Gertrude May, secretary of the senate, whom T. J. Toy had told me was Sloan Link's old flame.

I wandered over that way. A zealous doorkeeper attempted to stop me at the upper house door, but I pointed at the tiny pin I wore in my lapel and he grudgingly relented. They give us those pins so we can be recognized by the doormen. Most of the legislators won't wear them and give them away to favored people desiring entrance to the legislative floors, so the doorkeepers are suspicious of them. I'd even heard a story that in the session of last year a free enterpriser had figured the gimmick, bought quantities of pins like those that were issued, and made a brisk business out of selling those similars for a few bucks a throw.

I went in. My senator was in his seat staring dourly ahead. He does that better than he does anything else. He doesn't like me and I likewise him with interest. He belongs to the

Opposition and my defeated house opponent in the general election had been his best friend. They'd tottered around for a lot of sessions together. So he now only tolerates me carefully.

He nodded at me this day when I came up.

"Senator," I said humbly, "I need to meet Gertrude May."

"Hrrumphh," he said, with one of his seldom smiles. "I suspect I might arrange that." He made it sound like a great favor. He was eying me with more approval than normal. He made me remember my recent appointment and the fact that everyone sooner or later had bills in the Judiciary.

He took me back to a busy office behind the senate chambers. Harried girls worked typewriters, talked on telephones and scurried about on errands. A tall, handsome woman of early middle years issued haughty instructions and then retreated back into her office.

"That's Gertrude May," the senator said. "Follow me."

I followed him.

He introduced us, waited for a curious moment to see what I was about, and then retreated because I was pointedly waiting.

I eyed the woman behind the desk curiously. Her features were almost too delicate for prettiness, but her body was well made and well kept.

Her phone rang and she answered it, talked quickly, then hung it up.

"What did you want, Representative Robak?" she asked, her voice polite, impatience in her eyes.

"I've been appointed to a committee to look into the death of Representative Link. Your name was mentioned as an acquaintance of his," I said stiffly.

She nodded and her face relaxed a little. "I knew him. I dated him all last session." She smiled, almost to herself.

"I guess we were acquainted. A long time ago I thought we might get married." She shook her head. "He already had one wife. He was married to the Assembly. I never could keep him off Maker's Mark Bourbon long enough to make any binding promises to me. So it called itself off. We haven't been dating much this session. I never could get him anywhere but a bar." She grinned a gamin, loser's grin. "I tried to remember the other day, after I heard he was gone. In all of the times I went out with him I never went anywhere that there wasn't whiskey immediately available. We met in lobby rooms, taverns, bars. We never went to a show or to church or a play or a meeting. I never saw him on Sundays. The bars were closed. I suppose he was cuddled up next to a bottle those days." She shook her head again. "Maybe it was better company than I was."

"Did you see him the night he was killed?" I asked.

She nodded. "I suspect you know I saw him."

I smiled. "I do."

"Those are the words," she said, grinning. "Those are the ones I wanted him to say. 'I do.'" She looked away from me and came to some final decision. "We'd have been miserable, Don Robak. He was a drunk and I was his reformer. It wouldn't have lasted through the first cocktail hour. And now I'm sorry he's gone. I still turn around in the corridors outside because I think I see him, imagine I hear his voice. There were times I could have pushed him happily out his window, but I'm still sorry." She closed in combat with memories and didn't look up for a while. I waited and finally she realized I was still there and her eyes calculated me.

"This is your first session?" she asked.

I nodded.

"And chairman of an important committee. That's good."

She gave me wide eyes. "If you need any help, any advice, come see Momma Gertrude."

"I doubt that Momma Gertrude is any older than I am," I said, with some minor gallantry.

The eyes grew wider and then narrowed a bit. I felt I was being weighed and measured and found not completely wanting.

"Come have a drink with me sometime," she said. "I know where all of the bodies are buried, past and present. Together we can dig up a few."

"Sounds great," I said and nodded soothingly. "Please tell me about that last night you saw Link. Where was he and what was he doing?"

"He was in the downstairs bar in the Blue Hotel. It was maybe one o'clock in the morning. He was drunk. He was trying to get the barman to have the night bellman bring him a fresh bottle to his room. From what I caught, the night bellman was off servicing a big party at the Law-lobby room. So Sloan wound up talking the bartender out of a bottle himself." She nodded. "It's a violation of the liquor regulations, but the Blue will do it for an old customer if they think nothing will happen. Sloan was an old customer —I'll say that."

"Maker's Mark whiskey?" I asked.

"Sure," she said. "There wasn't any other kind for him." She touched her finely carved lips with a finger and said musingly: "When he first got elected to the house he didn't even know what good whiskey was. He was a moonshine-and-cheap-blend man."

"Was anyone with him in the bar?"

She shook her head. "No. Unless you want to count me. I tried to talk to him. He brushed me off, left me standing there. He was drunk."

"What did you talk to him about?"

She looked away from me. "There wasn't any talk. I tried to say something to him and he charged past me as if I wasn't alive any more. He'd written me off like a bad year." She leaned forward against the desk. I expected tears, but none came. "That's all there was," she said tonelessly.

I wasn't sure she was telling me all of it, but I nodded. "Okay, Mrs. May. Thank you for talking to me."

"Don't call me Mrs. May," she said. "Mr. May's dead five years now. Call me Gertrude or Gert. No one calls me Trudy." She veiled the eyes a little. "Come have a drink with me sometime soon, Don. Promise?"

I promised and made my way on out and back to the house side. In the rotunda, lobbyists hailed me as if I'd been lost all session and they were suddenly glad they'd found me. I saw T. J. Toy wheedling a senator, but he must have missed me, for he wouldn't or didn't look my way.

They still weren't in session in the house. I walked past pages who were working at being busy and finally I sat in my seat. My desk was stacked with mail and those letters reminded me of something. I'd forgotten the letters I'd taken from Sloan's desk.

I couldn't remember for a moment what I'd done with them. I cudgeled my memory, had a sudden inspiration, reached in my inside coat pocket and they were there. There were two of them. One of them was in a neatly typed envelope with no return address. The other was more interesting. It was addressed to Sloan in clumsy block letters. It was stamped fore and aft with a red stamp that boldly said: USE THE NAME OF CHRIST WHEN YOU PRAY. I thought about postal penalties for a moment or two and then opened it.

It read: "I kno your out the windo ded you never did

59

anithin for ani one and you shud hav ded a long time now your kil you stinc basturd."

It wasn't signed, but the writer had managed to stamp it three times inside with the red stamp bearing the same legends that were stamped on the envelope. The letter was postmarked on the day after Sloan had died. I carefully put it back in the envelope. I got out the other and thought about opening it also, but then decided I'd better run it up to Captain Carlson. I hoped I hadn't messed up any fingerprints.

The letter mildly excited me. It was badly written, but there was that "kil" part in it. No one knew Link had been killed on the day it was mailed.

I left my own mail and went to the house telephone center and had one of the operators that I knew call Carlson's office.

She reported that he wasn't in yet, so I left a message for him to call.

I went back into the house chambers and sat again in my tall wing chair that hid me effectively from all behind me. I picked idly at my own mail. Down in the stack something appeared that electrified me. There was an envelope addressed to me in familiar block letters. And, on the front and back of the envelope, there was stamped in red ink: USE THE NAME OF CHRIST WHEN YOU PRAY.

I felt a rush of exultation. If I'd messed up prints on the one to Link it looked as if I was getting a second chance. I separated the letter from the rest of my mail and put it in my coat pocket along with the letters to Link.

The house still hadn't convened when Captain Carlson returned my call. I took the elevator to the top floor of the Statehouse and made my way down dark corridors and past racks of rusting spittoons. Here and there an employee pushed a broom against the dust of time.

I presented the letters to Carlson.

"This one's been opened," he said suspiciously.

"Sure," I said. "Here's another from the same guy, looks like. This second one is to me. I didn't open it." I pointed at the Link letter. "There's that 'kil' in there that's kind of suspicious considering the date it was mailed. And the writer is undoubtedly a psycho."

He shrugged. "Okay," he said, "we'll check them all out for prints. Maybe that will tell us something. We should have something on it by the first of the week." He sighed and regarded me dolefully. Outside, pigeons made boisterous landings on the roof. "You're keeping me in business. Anything else?"

I nodded. "On his last night Link was on the town with T. J. Toy, who's a jackleg lobbyist. Toy claims he left him at midnight or thereabouts." I carefully went through what I'd learned from Toy and Gertrude May. "Maybe Toy ought to be checked out also," I finished.

"Okay," he said, when I was done. "I hear you have a knack for this. I talked to your police chief down there in Bington. George Gentrup. I know him pretty well. He said, among other things, that you're stubborn, opinionated and that I should watch my billfold and not odd man you for coffee." He grinned. "He said you're okay for a lawyer, which is a left-handed compliment. He told me to tell you to keep your legs crossed and stay sober here in the big city."

"George Gentrup's a good horse," I said quickly. "He likes almost anyone who doesn't try to steal his wife. He hasn't caught me yet. I have a quick bicycle."

"Sure you do," he said without smiling. "What now?"

"While you're doing your checking I'll try that black-and-tan place tonight."

He frowned. "I could probably do better than you getting information out of that place."

61

I shook my head. "I've got an 'in' there. If you want to double-check it afterwards that would be okay, but please wait until I've checked it out."

"What do you have going?" he asked curiously.

"A black legislator who knows the owner. He's going with me. And the owner is impressed by politicians."

He nodded. "All that could help."

"How about you?" I asked. "Have you run onto anything new?"

He fumbled through his file and brought out a long list. "Here's a list of the legislative bills that weren't present in Link's room. I'd like to have you look it over. Maybe it'll mean something to you. It doesn't mean anything to me." He handed me the list and I stuffed it in my inside pocket.

He got out a pencil and wrote something on the file. "Another thing," he said. "I'll check out the Blue Hotel and see what I can find out in the bar." He shook his head. "Selling booze by the bottle. They oughtn't to do that. It bends the law. Maybe I can get some information out of them by doing a little winking at the violation."

"Captain," I said in a horrified voice, "what you suggest borders on subornation."

For the first time he looked at me as if he liked me and smiled.

I smiled back.

"There's one more thing, Don," he said slowly. "This *friend* of yours has killed one man. Maybe he'll try for another. You'd be a likely candidate."

"Maybe," I said.

"You want a gun? I can fix it up. I can even supply one for you."

I shook my head. "No. I don't like guns. They make me nervous."

62

"You were in the war weren't you?"

"Yes."

"Combat?"

I nodded.

He shrugged. "I never argue with a man who's made up his mind. But the invitation remains open."

The house was in busy session when I returned. They were fighting it out on a warm one for a welcome change. This one was a tax bill.

My state operates off a number of different revenues. There's gasoline tax, inheritance tax, intangibles tax, property tax, income tax, corporate tax and, lately, a sales tax. Each merchant collects this sales tax from customers by adding it to the bill for items purchased. When the law was originally passed it was decided that persons who sold only "services" wouldn't have to collect or add the additional sales-tax percentage onto his bill.

And so the fun began. Doctors, lawyers, barbers didn't have to collect sales tax. Everyone wanted to scramble on the same wagon. Moving picture theaters and places of amusement, such as race tracks, commercial parks and camp grounds filed suits against the tax, claiming they were renderers of service. State auto dealers screamed that they were losing sales to nearby states with lesser sales tax. Grocers decided that food, because it was a necessity, shouldn't be taxed. Druggists got indignant over collecting it on the sale of medicines.

So now, for the umpteenth time, the house was deciding what was subject to the tax. The infighting was deadly.

With this going on, the house was only about three-fourths full. Some legislators were "skating." That meant they'd decided that things would wax hot for them no matter which way they voted, so they just weren't going to be around when the voting roll was called.

There's a bar right across the street from the legislature. Sloan Link used to claim that a wise and provident God placed it there for the benefit of thirsty legislators. Over the years it's become such a gathering place for reluctant-to-vote legislators that they now call it the "Skating Rink."

I sat back in my chair and listened to the arguments. I'd already made up my mind to vote against any group seeking exemption.

I wondered who Sloan Link had let into his room. I pondered on what had been interesting enough to get him to go out of his room and refuel on Maker's Mark to share with a shadowy killer.

It sounded as if it could have been a woman. Knowing Sloan's morality or lack of it I thought he'd have let a woman into his room at the drop of a brassiere strap.

He was a big man. It would have taken a strong woman to kill him and then lift that ponderous body out of the window. Gertrude May looked strong. She'd admitted the desire to kill him, but wasn't that hate half a love thing?

She was the last one who'd seen him that I knew about so far, but she'd admitted the seeing readily. I had the feeling she'd have run back to Sloan anytime he'd given a casual lift to one of his massive eyebrows.

There was always T. J. Toy. He'd been out with Link earlier. Link might have opened the door to him.

There were other shadows still unknown.

There were legislators. I hated to believe that one of Sloan's colleagues could have done it.

And yet . . .

The Speaker brought me up out of it by banging his gavel

hard against his podium and adjourning the house for lunch. That left the tax bill still to be voted on in the afternoon.

George Chapell, the minority leader, got up from his seat, stretched and yawned, and caught my eye.

"Press Club it?" he called.

I nodded.

We gathered a crew of legislators and headed for the Press Club. The chili there is vaguely edible and the cheeseburgers are constructed more out of cheese than hamburger, but, as a set-off, they serve the biggest, iciest martinis in town.

Remembering my plumpening physique I ordered only the chili and had three martinis instead of two, hoping my stomach would be stunned into not noticing the lack of food.

Chapell sat next to me.

"How's the hunt going?" he asked.

"Fair," I said. I didn't really think he was interested, but I went on: "Have you had a chance to talk to Ed Polsen today?"

He shook his head in negation. "I've been fighting it out on this damn tax bill all morning."

I vaguely filled him in on what had happened to date, leaving out my own conjectures and what I planned for the evening and keeping the report low key.

"Go hard," he said when I was done. "Just don't get in any trouble. I don't think Ed will help you out and I damn well know I won't."

I looked at him. His face was cold.

"Your choice," I said. "I've been bailing myself out of my own messes for thirty-odd years. I'll try to get by if help's refused now."

"Police ought to be doing what you're doing—if they had any police up around here worth a damn."

I leaned toward him, getting a little angrier. "I'll go

through it once more. Some of the stuff I'm getting would take the police a lot more time and a lot more digging than it's taking me. Captain Carlson's not unhappy." I watched him closely. "Why are you?"

"I think the whole affair's stupid," he said harshly. "We've had legislators die up here before. So now, in the first session where your people have been in charge in many years, suddenly along comes a big smell because some loose legislator goes out a window."

"What do you mean by loose?" I asked quietly.

He shrugged eloquently. His eyes were morose. "I'm not going into that with you. You were one of his boys. What jerks me is that we've had a half-dozen legislators commit suicide since I've been around up here. At least that many more have been accidentally killed. A hell of a lot more than that have just plain died. We never had to have cops around on those."

"Captain Carlson believes that someone threw Link out the window after beating his head in. I have no reason not to believe it happened that way. Do you think the police are lying about it?"

He sneered. "In this city? Could be, Donnie, could be."

"That's martini talk," I said, still irritated.

He shook his head. "No. Just wait until you've been around this place as long as I have. This is a crooked town. The cops here are crooked. They also hate us and fear us. When we're around the word goes out. The rough stuff is out, the bookie joints and the high-rolling places close. Their income dies and their work doubles." He smiled without humor. "Four years ago a legislator sued the city and a policeman for arresting him. He won. They know now they can't even arrest us except for felony and treason. They knew it before, but until they were sued they ignored it." He looked

66

away from me. "I know some of them up here who are crooked enough to do anything." He looked back at me. "You believe it your way and I'll believe it mine. My belief comes from experience. You won't change me. I think the Capitol City police have faked up what you're looking into, faked it for purposes of their own. I think the committee is a waste of time. I think you're poking and prodding where you shouldn't. Give it up, Don."

I watched him. He was red faced, angry. Fortunately for my own temper and his, the waitress picked that time to bring our third martinis.

He smiled a small smile and picked his up, waited for me to raise mine, then tapped glasses.

"Hell, do what you want," he said with some restoration of temper. "I should be happy. I'm on liberty today. My wife went home for the weekend." He grinned slyly. "I told her I'd have to stay here. Press of work, you know."

I remembered his blond wife. She was always expensively garbed, made-up and perfumed, but I believed her to be as cold as an Alaskan winter. I suspected she spent more time primping at a mirror than she spent in bed at fundamentals. Maybe mirrors told her she was: Fairest of them all.

If they did so tell her, then they lied. I lifted my glass to him. "Confusion to the opposition," I said.

"Doesn't quite fit," he said, "but the sentiment's just right." He looked at me carefully. "I like you again, Robak."

"Thank you," I said.

The conversation went to the tax bill. Everyone at the table got into the talk on that.

CHAPTER VI

RULE 14. *Members of the General Assembly are expected and required to act with decorum and courtesy during the session. All violations shall be reported. . . .*

That afternoon the house adjourned at a little after four. None of the heavy-pressure groups desiring exclusion from the tax bill had made it, which pleased me.

I imagined it worried some lobbyists, such as T. J. Toy.

I went to the room I'd picked for the Judiciary meeting and waited.

And waited.

And waited. Ho hum.

After a while I went back down to the blackboard, thinking I'd made a mistake and gone to the wrong room.

There were a lot of signs for meetings chalked on the blackboard, but mine wasn't one of them. That irritated me. I'd heard of it happening before. Someone doesn't want a committee to meet, so he or she rubs out the notice of that meeting. Sloan Link had told me about sharpies doing that. It was an effective weapon late in the session.

It wasn't that late in the session and Sloan had also given me the antidote.

Monday would be soon enough. And this time I'd make sure there was a meeting.

I went to the Law lobby and had a couple of drinks to reduce my blood pressure. Then I went on to my own room and called Judy.

We preliminaried a bit and then I said: "I'm going to George's Rendezvous with Fred Olean to check some stuff out we picked up last night. You can go along if you want to. I hear the place is a little wild."

I could almost see her shudder. "I believe I'll pass tonight, Don. Are you going down to Bington for the weekend when you're done then?"

"Either tonight or in the morning." I remembered that Governor Bratewell had given me a message for my partner, ex-Senator Adams. "I've some things to do down there."

"I'll see you Monday, then?" she asked.

"Maybe even Sunday night," I said enouraged.

"Remember that you're taking me to Governor Bratewell's reception Monday," she said.

"I remember," I said, remembering again.

I rehung the phone and looked at my watch. I wasn't supposed to meet Fred Olean for a few hours.

I walked up to the Athletic Club and worked out and then took a swim. I felt tired instead of healthy when I was done. The trip did have some value. Upstairs I managed to make friends with a talkative bell captain. He knew T. J. Toy and had been on duty the night Link was killed. He checked out the other members of his staff who'd been around that night after I gave him five dollars. No one could verify that T. J. Toy had ever come in that night and no one could say he hadn't.

At nine o'clock I met Fred Olean in the lobby of the Blue. He inspected me and found much wanting. "You look beat, Don," he commented. "I was going to suggest we walk out. It's only a few blocks." He shook his head. "I'm putting on weight. I need the exercise."

"If you desire exercise," I said mournfully, "then you can come with me to the Athletic Club next week. I went there this afternoon and I'm shot down, stiff, beat and sore from the experience. Tonight we ride a cab on me." I looked at his smile. "If you insist on exercise you can carry me piggyback to the door from the cab."

"Carry you?" he questioned. "Just how big are you, Robek?"

"Larger than I should be. Six foot plus, weighing in at two-ought-five, which is ten pounds over normal."

He looked surprised. "That's just what I've gained."

I nodded. "It's the Athletic Club for you, Olean."

George's Rendezvous wasn't very busy for a Friday night. Places like George's are beginning to pass away. If things aren't better now, then they at least are different. It used to be that you had to put out a sign that gave evidence that both blacks and whites were welcome.

George's had signboards in front showing black entertainers. The gentleman in the tails, who ushered us to seats, was black. The waitress was black, but she was living in the Playboy manner. Her costume was short and had a bunny tail.

The sparse crowd was mixed. So, observed Fred Olean, were he and I. Our table was near the stage.

"Wait patiently," Fred said. "George will be along."

I nodded and we ordered a drink from the hop-a-long waitress. It came quickly, but was only decently touched with Bourbon, and overpriced.

A very large black man came into the bar of the place from some almost hidden door. He shook hands up and down the bar with customers, then peered into the larger room where we sat. He spied Fred, waved, and came over quickly when Fred beckoned to him.

"Governor," he said to Fred, who stood up and shook hands with him.

"I want you to meet Don Robak, who's in the house with me," Fred said.

George nodded, but didn't offer a hand, although the nod seemed friendly. He inspected me.

Fred said: "He's the only soul brother I know bred of a Polack daddy and an Irish mother. He's a lawyer out of Bington. Don't hold being a lawyer against him. Someone has to do it and it might as well be the mentally defective."

George grinned openly at me. He was huge, but he wasn't gross. I figured his height at about eight inches over the six-foot mark and his weight at near three hundred. He looked like one of those great tough ones you see up in the line for the pro teams. He had one of the trademarks of that group of athletes, a pointed beard, now slightly graying. He looked tough and competent. I guessed his age at plus forty.

"I've heard a little about you," he said. "You took Link's old job after he got killed." He nodded. "I knew Link. He was one of my favorites." He held out an arm, massive as a tree. "See this. Link and I used to arm wrestle and we were so close that sometimes I'd win and sometimes he'd win."

"Was he in here the night he was killed?"

George looked hard at Fred Olean. Olean nodded. "Sit down, George," he said. "I wouldn't have brought him in here if I didn't want you to talk to him."

George grinned and sat down. "He was here," he said. "That T. J. Toy brought him in. It was a sort of busy night.

There were some other guys from the house around and they all sat together and T.J. picked up the tab."

"Who were the others?"

He shrugged. "A bunch. Maybe a dozen. Speaker Mc-Guire, George Chapell, Ed Polsen and some others." He named them without hesitation. "Then there were four or five from the senate, but they weren't sitting with T.J. He sent them some drinks over." He named the senators also.

"Anything happen while Link was in here? Anything out of the way?"

He shook his head. It was more an act of remembering than of negation. "Link'd been drinking. He was complaining about the weather. It was cold out that night. He said the older he got the colder he got. Only way he could stay warm up here was booze." He snapped his massive fingers. "There was one thing I almost forgot. I had to throw out some kid that came bothering around Link. Some punk named Cisco or Lesco or something like that. He went over to the table and tried to get something going with Link. Got real, real nasty."

"Would the name have been Joe Metzco?" I asked, knowing with a prickling feeling that it would be.

"That's it. He was some kid. He wasn't one of the long hairs. Had his hair cut real short, like you used to see kids have it. Burrhead. Don't see much of that these days."

I nodded. "He's a bottle of poison. He runs a far Right group down on campus. They call themselves the Alones." I took a sip of my drink. "For every action there's a reaction."

Fred said brightly, "You sure are full of those bright sayings."

I grinned, although I didn't feel like it. "Metzco is sick Right. He wants to see martial law for purposes of his own. He wants all of the long hairs killed. He hates us all,

73

Catholics, Jews, Protestants, blacks, whites, yellows, reds. He believes the world can survive only if we cut the population to a few million. Then, I think he wants the survivors to hunt each other for food." I looked over at Fred Olean. "In a college town you get every kind of kook. This one ran in the primary down there in Bington, along with nine, count them, nine others. My opponents. Metzco only got seventy-three votes, but every time I see him I still get the shivers. I don't know why he ran. He isn't for anything. He's only against things. Burn them and kill them."

"But I'll bet he thought he was going to win," Fred said softly. "Something always convinces them."

"I guess maybe he did," I said. "He used to have a peculiar smile for me, as if he knew something I didn't know." I shook my head. "I didn't know he was up here in Capitol City."

George shook his own head. "He told the bouncer he was just here for the day and was going back to Bington."

"I better check him out over the weekend," I said.

"Wouldn't he have hated Sloan Link?" Fred asked.

"He hates everyone. Sloan was carrying some things that Metzco would be for. I'm sure he'd be for the tuition hike because most of the other students are against it. He'd figure that if it passed it might bring some sort of outbreak that he'd hope would be put down bloodily. He'd be for any bill that would cause upheaval, against any that might solve problems or make life easier." I looked at George. "You have any idea what he was snapping about at Link?"

"No. I got there when the name calling began. Link wanted to fight him. Metzco was willing. I think he thought Link was drunk enough he could maybe handle him." He shook his head. "Link wasn't that drunk."

"Funny that T.J. didn't remember that," I said.

74

He laughed. "T.J. didn't know whether he was pitching or catching by that time."

I nodded. "Did any of the other legislators leave with T.J. and Link?"

"I don't think so," he said. He looked restlessly around. Someone signaled him from another table. He waved.

"Someone shoved him out the window later that night. I'm interested in everything that happened to him. If you think of anything else at all, give Fred a call and he'll get it to me," I said.

He held out his hand and enveloped the one I thrust into it. He nodded at me with minor approval, patted Fred's broad back, and table-hopped away.

We sipped our drinks and the bunny-tailed waitress was diligent with refills. The entertainment began. The first act was a black stripper, beautifully built, extremely acrobatic. When she'd discarded a lot more clothes than I thought she'd originally worn they switched the lights off. On her thin tights phosphorescent hands were painted strategically. She got some action out of that.

When the lights came back up and the applause died Fred tapped me subtly and pointed with a guarded gesture.

"Look over there," he said.

George Chapell was sitting at a table in the darkest part of the room. He was with a creamy, brown-skinned girl.

"I know who she is," Fred said. "She's a professional. T. J. Toy's been using her now and then."

"Chapell's wife would surely kill him," I said.

"Only if one of us rats on him," Fred said. "Squeak, squeak."

"You don't like him much do you, Fred?"

Fred smiled. "He's pretty much of an ass. He's the kind I wish they'd segregate me from." He shook his head, impatient with his own statement. "I don't really dislike him. It's just that there isn't any sand in him. I've never found anyplace I can stand without sinking farther."

I nodded amiably.

We sat there and had a few more. I knew I was going to have to drive to Bington, my home, but after the few I decided that it might be brighter to wait, sleep the night in the hotel, then drive down sober after an early call. That way I could still get down to Bington in the morning before the office opened.

So, on the excuse of watching Chapell, we had one more and then one more than that. And I looked around after a considerable time and discovered that Chapell and his date were gone.

Fred laughed a little. "They left sometime back. I was wondering when you'd notice."

I grimaced. "We'd better get out of here while I'm still uptight enough to limp to a cab."

He nodded. "Right you are. If they really put anything in those drinks we'd both be rolling down the hill." He leaned forward. "Maybe it would interest you to know that Chapell left after he noticed us. He seemed to be having a good time and then he spotted us. I doubt he expected to see anyone around on a Friday night when we're adjourned for the weekend. When he did spot us he no less than hauled freight quick."

Before we could leave, the girl with the phosphorescent hands came back, so we watched her act with clinical interest.

Then we cabbed back to the Blue.

With all of that exercise and the many drinks I slept like a baby, without dreams.

But with my door double-locked.

CHAPTER VII

RULE 16. *All members shall be allowed mileage for necessary travel at the rate of 8¢ per mile and shall . . .*

In the morning I did arise early. I carefully coddled my ancient Plymouth, which had been enjoying the luxury of a heated garage, down the Bington road. I made it before nine o'clock.

I came in town on the River Road, which overlooks Bington and borders the state university. Students hurried to Saturday classes or walked somewhere briskly in the cold. I parked downtown. The streets seemed quiet after Capitol City. People smiled at each other and two or three strollers waved to me and I waved back happily.

The storefronts were old and the sidewalks uncrowded. Even the temperature seemed warmer than it had been in Capitol City. I reflected on the sane sameness of my small town. There's a stability in the mere act of seeing the same people and in doing the same tasks each day. That stability was temporarily missing from my life and I missed it.

In my small town you know who is untrustworthy, who you can like and dislike. In the legislature I knew that the

77

faces worn by short-term acquaintances were still hidden.

I enjoyed a cup of coffee and basketball talk in Mac's Coffee Shop and then went on to the office. Virginia, our aging, temperamental typist-secretary, was massaging her electric with determined fingers when I arrived at the office. She frowned at me and I remembered what she'd told me when I'd the temerity to ask for her vote. I knew that she was a stanch member of that other party. Her last real interest in it, however, had died when the senator, my law partner, got out of active politics, but her reaction remained. She told me: "I'd as soon vote for a yellow dog as vote for a member of your party." I hadn't even drawn a smile with the statement. I doubted I had gotten her vote.

"Good morning, Mr. Representative Robak," she said. "How nice of you to honor us. There's a lot of mail I wish you'd clear from your desk." She thumbed a notebook. "Several people have called and wanted to know where you were." She grinned stolidly. "I told them nothing, figuring it might hurt business with you playing about in that mess up there."

"Thank you for protecting me," I said, voice serious. "Is the senator in yet?"

She nodded. "He has some appointments later on, but no one is due until about ten o'clock." She condescended. "Go on in."

I tapped at his door and went on in. He was laid back in his swivel chair, feet up on his desk. He's an old, thin man, and he was deep now in the law, happily researching away. I know for certain, after my short years of practice, that I'll never have his inquiring gift. For me the practice is a chore, a job. He loves it, lives it, vacations it, eats and sleeps it. Now he is getting old and his hands tremble sometimes when he picks at the heavy legal books, but he will die doing what he loves, on his feet and not cowering somewhere in bed.

Since his wife passed on, his only real pleasure is the law, although he'll take an occasional Bourbon and branch water when the hour is late and his eyes are tired.

He picked at a strand of white hair and peered up at me over his glasses.

"Ah, Representative Robak," he said. He eyed me keenly with a tiny trace of humor. "I see by the local paper that you've been appointed chairman of what they term a 'powerful committee.' Have you returned to Bington to oppress us?"

I grinned at him. Then I sat down on his old leather couch.

"The governor asked about you," I said. "I think he wants you up in Capitol City to act as a liaison between his office and the legislature. He'd like for you to call him if you can see your way clear." I shook my head. "I didn't make any commitment for you."

He contemplated what I'd said for a moment. "Maybe I should do that." He leaned back in his chair. "I don't get up to Capitol City much these days. Perhaps I hate to admit, even to myself, that I miss it." He looked at me. "Do you like it, Don?"

"Yes," I said slowly, looking for the right way to say it. "More than anything I've ever done. I think I could be good at it in time."

He nodded. "I think you could also." He looked away. "I'll clean up what I've got to do, get a few things continued, and come on up to keep you out of mischief. I've read also that you're up to ancient tricks—named to a group investigating a murder."

"That's right," I said, without inflection. I watched him closely. "You knew Sloan Link, didn't you?"

He nodded. "Over two or three sessions, I got to know

79

him fairly well. I suppose that you were fond of him. Most people were until they knew him well. I wasn't by the time we parted. In my opinion he was one of those rare ones who view themselves as the only real and important people, the only ones worth worrying about. Everyone and everything else is merely something to be dealt with." He nodded again, almost to himself. "He was a damn good legislator though. He taught himself to be one. He knew the rules and he knew how to use them. He was pretty effective. Most legislators never learn them, so it winds up being about ten per cent of the lads up there who actually plan and run things. The others only vote." He smiled at me. "I trust you're one of the ten per cent."

"I'll never admit it and I doubt that anyone, up to now, ever thought so. I've wandered along, but I've gotten smarter," I said. "At least I hope I've gotten smarter. How about some of the other powers in the house? Do you know any of them?"

He knuckled a prodigious memory. "Let's see, the minority leader. Wouldn't that be George Chapell?" He nodded, answering his own question. "Sure. He's been around up there for a lot of years. I know him. My wife and his wife were . . . acquaintances . . . not friends. I doubt that any female was ever a friend to that wife of George's. She spends her life hunting pedestals she can look down from, except maybe that one time in Link's first term." He tapped on the desk with a sharp pencil. "She went head over for Sloan Link. Didn't last long. I heard Sloan ran her off. She went back to George and she had all of that money, so George took her back. George is all right if you can stand his caliber, which must be considerably less than .22."

"What's wrong with him?" I asked, puzzled. "He's got a sort of a bad temper and he chases a little, but I think he's funny most of the time. You're the second reputable person who's bad-mouthed him in the last twelve hours."

"His word isn't good and he forgets his promises. Those are very bad legislative traits." He looked at me and his eyes were old and wise. "Don't do any trading with him, Don, unless he has to deliver his part of the trade first."

"I'll remember," I said.

"I don't know the people on your side of the aisle as well as I know my own. The fat man, Speaker McGuire, is reputed to be a pretty tough politician. There was a bit of scandal about him some years back, something about a campaign contribution that went awry and into his personal pocket, but it must have blown over. He never got indicted or tried and he keeps getting elected. I hear around that he badly wants to move on up, maybe run for U. S. Senator next time."

"How about Ed Polsen?"

"I don't recall him being there when I was there. I know him a little. He's a real personality boy, right able. I tried a case against him a few years back. He was well set up and did a good job."

"Where does he practice?" I asked.

He shook his head. "He's got a law degree. I don't think he's involved in the practice. He's some kind of investment counselor. He appeared as a witness as to damages for the other side." He looked away and then back. "He wasn't very careful with the truth on the witness stand, like most of you politicians. He was a good witness though. Stayed right with it, couldn't get him to change his story. I suppose he had some kind of percentage going in the case."

"Who won?" I asked.

He grinned. "I like to believe that I did. It was a rather complicated condemnation suit. A jury gave his people a little less than we'd offered to settle. I had the feeling that maybe Polsen and his trial counsel maybe went ahead and tried the case because of getting a bigger percentage on trial than they would have gotten on settlement. He was about like most of us wind-up, I suppose. Hungry, short of money."

"Anything else you can think of?" I asked.

He shrugged. "Probably not. Anyone who's managed to survive in the political jungles of this state is sure to have some mat burns. If you check into any of those guys you'll find troubles, but that doesn't mean they'd murder someone."

"Was T. J. Toy up there when you were around?"

He shook his head. "The name doesn't mean anything to me. Who is he?"

"A lobbyist. Wears beautiful clothes. This time he's working against the anti-pollution bill."

"I can't place him."

"How about Gertrude May. She's secretary of the senate? Did you know her?"

He nodded with some enthusiasm. "Gert's first-class people. Got a heart as big as a hotel. Mouth that's only slightly smaller. When I was up there she was going with Senator Sebring. That was in between husband one and husband two. Later, I heard she was dating your deceased compatriot, Representative Link. I suppose they were living somewhat fatly on Link's money." He looked away. "She was a handsome woman when I knew her."

"She still is," I said, remembering. "What's this about Link's money? I didn't know he had any."

He shrugged. "Let's say he lived pretty well on his income. That's the kindest way I can put it."

I digested that. Whether he was on the take or not, Link

had convinced the senator, who was a pretty astute judge of human behavior.

"You have anything concrete on that?" I asked.

He hesitated for a moment. "Now and then someone pulls a real deal up in the legislature. Someone will come along who has some power and offer a new tax bill to tax, for example, beer. Then the beer people get all up in arms. Maybe someone gets the word to them that the bill just might die if the right amount of money is paid to the right person. When the bill's author was Link, sometimes it did die. Those kind of bills got proposed by Link too many times and died too many times." He looked at me. "Anti-pollution might have been his newest gambit. Maybe it wasn't meant for anything but show. Maybe Link was riding it until the time was right to sell it out."

I considered that for a long moment. It had an interesting sound. I've been wrong about people too many times to not believe that I could have been wrong about Link. Oddly, even if he'd been on the take, it didn't change my feeling about him. I'd liked him.

I looked back at the senator. "Do you think you could get done what you need to get done and ride up with me tomorrow evening early?"

He inclined his head. "I could try. Give me a little time on the telephone today and I just might. I'll start by calling the governor."

"When you get up there," I said, "I'd appreciate it if you sniffed around and found out whether or not Link was on the take on anti-pollution."

He nodded. "All I can do is try," he said. "Did you ever think that he might have been smoke screening on that and looking elsewhere for a bundle?"

"That's a thought," I said.

I left him there, with Virginia trying to raise the governor for him by telephone.

I went into my own office and no one came in for a while and there was room to think a little about the whole messy picture.

Tonight I'd try to track down Joe Metzco, the Rightist student leader, erstwhile primary foe. He was insane enough, I decided, to do away with anyone who didn't agree with him, if he thought he'd go undetected. I really considered him to be a deranged person without any contact or understanding of the world around him.

I doubted his ability, though, to obtain entrance into Sloan's room. Maybe he'd waited until Sloan was drunk and then gained admittance. It seemed far fetched, but once inside he could have smashed in Sloan's head, pushed him out the window, then made an unseen escape. The crime fitted Metzco. It was savage, but with luck and the right breaks could have been considered an accident.

There was also at least the possibility that some other psycho had done it. The crank letter I'd opened, despite its lack of understandability, could have been from someone who, prior to the release of the news, knew and rejoiced in the fact that Sloan had been murdered.

Also I had to take into the reckoning one Gertrude May. Perhaps her heart was broken, but it wasn't too broken to look around for Sloan's successor. I hated to think of her as a murderess because she was bright and able and handsome, but handsome, bright, able women sometimes kill.

Then a hundred legislators, led by Speaker McGuire, George Chapell and Ed Polsen, were possibles. Maybe it was someone who was in the house or *had* been in the house who hated Link for a matter I'd not yet uncovered.

Most important and what I kept coming back to was T. J.

Toy. No matter what Captain Carlson found out, I needed to do a little in-depth study on T.J. when I returned to Capitol City.

After a while I could quit restlessly mulling it. A female client came in. Her husband was out of work, drunk, behind on his support payments to a previous wife, and mean to his children by my client. Together we tried to plot a way out of all that. It was difficult.

After that there was a man who wanted to file a suit because a friend had borrowed five hundred dollars from him and not repaid him. Questioning brought out that this friend was out of work, drunk, behind on his support payments to two ex-wives. I never did find out whether or not he was mean to his children.

And so went Saturday morning. . . .

That night I located Joe Metzco in a near campus bar called the Orangeman. It was an ancient, dingy place that I'd once frequented during my own campus time. I doubted anyone had cleaned it since I'd left school. It featured cool, but not cold, draft beer, stringy pizza, and enough darkness to hide minor sins. Once I was inside I remembered the darkness. That was why I'd once liked it.

Metzco was drinking there with one of his several lieutenants. I got three fresh bottles of beer and brought them over to his table.

He eyed me without alarm. "Sir Representative," he said softly, lip curling.

I sat down across from him and his lieutenant. The lieutenant, who had his hair all shaved off, sneered openly at me.

Metzco smiled. I seemed to have caught him in a benevolent mood or he wanted to examine me like a bug. He nodded at the other boy. "Go someplace for a while," he

85

said in that soft voice that he must have picked up from a Bogart revival.

The kid snatched the extra beer resentfully and strode stiffly away.

"What brings the establishment in here?" Metzco asked, after the boy was gone.

"Maybe I'm just calling on constituents," I said.

He was without humor. He looked me over coolly, eyes wary, muscled arms tensing and relaxing.

"What do you want, Robak? There must be something? I lost all desire to see you after last primary." He looked away from me. "I could have given them some fun up there, maybe even have done them good. I could have told them, made them believe." He looked back at me, his voice and eyes hypnotic. "You must see it, Robak. There isn't anything left for government. It's a tottering wreck, an animal with a death wound. It would be mercy to kill it. There are too many people for it to work any more. Men have become dirty little fleas on the back of this dead-dog world. We've poisoned it all. Only when men are dead will the world come back, clean itself. Even the seas are full of pollution. There isn't a clean place left."

"I've got an answer for you, Metzco," I said, making my voice as soft as his. He waited so I gave it to him: "Build yourself a time machine and go back to the days of Attila the Hun."

It passed over him. He touched my sleeve. "No one ever dies, Robak. You come back as something else when you die, maybe a bird or a dog or an insect. But something's happened to the ratios. They've gone insane. Even with all of the killings and the wars there are too many of us and too few of the others. Maybe that's the way it's supposed to end with all of us strangling in our excrement." He con-

templated that thought, watching the dirty ceiling with eyes
that failed to see it or me and I waited for a long moment
and then touched his arm.

"Metzco," I said. Then louder: "Metzco!"

He shook himself back to a world that he didn't compre-
hend and which didn't understand him and his eyes finally
focused on me.

"What was your problem with Sloan Link?"

"I saw you were on that committee." He looked away and
his voice went to low-low. "Link and I had no problems."

"Not true. I hear you got into a shouting match with him
in a bar in Capitol City the same night he went out a
window. I thought I'd give you the courtesy of telling me
about it instead of the police."

He shrugged. "Anti-pollution," he said. "He had a bill in
up there that would have slowed the rush down." He held up
a hand and examined it wonderingly. "It wouldn't have
stopped it, but it would have slowed it. So I got on him." He
shook his head. "I thought he was one of my brothers. Here
he had this really great tuition bill and then he has a stupid
thing like anti-pollution. I tried to tell him about it and he
started shouting at me. Then a couple of darkies take me
by the neck and I'm out of there." He smiled grimly, surely.
"I'll go back sometime very soon with a couple of fire
bombs."

I nodded. "Undoubtedly that would solve all problems,"
I said. I watched him carefully and thought he maybe would
remember me also with a fire bomb, but I could always over-
insure. Besides he was making my lower backside ache and
even if he still gave me a chill it was running south of where
it had run before.

"You really think the world should commit suicide, don't
you, Metzco?"

"Something like that," he said, letting his voice go back to that affected, hypnotic monotone.

I nodded. "Lead them then. Go first. Be a pathfinder."

He recoiled a little from me. I got up slowly, waiting for him to say something, but he remained silent. His thin buddy watched us from the bar uncomprehending.

I left them there to plot together.

CHAPTER VIII

RULE 18. *Members of the General Assembly shall be allowed per diem expenses to defray living costs during the sessions.*

The next night I checked my law partner into the Blue Hotel. A room had been found for him there without any great trouble after a friendly call from the governor's office.

"Looks the same," he said. He stared around as we waited for one of the hotel's elusive bellhops. He pointed up to a dark corner of the vaulted, three-story-high lobby. "See up there?"

I looked, but saw nothing. Shadows.

"Same cobwebs that were up there ten years ago," he said darkly. "I'll bet that spider's as big as a basket now and is so spoiled it won't eat anything but fat politicians." He nodded and inspected me carefully. "About twenty more pounds for you, Donald." He nodded again. "Right out of a bad horror movie is the Blue Hotel lobby."

"Enjoy it while you can," I said. "They're tearing it down to make a parking garage."

"Huzzah! Huzzah!" he called, while the room clerk

watched both of us carefully for other outward signs of insanity.

The bellhop came and rescued the room clerk. I got off on my floor after making arrangements to meet the senator in half an hour.

I cleaned up and tried to call Judy from the room, but there wasn't any answer, although I let the phone ring for a long time.

I sat in my comfortable chair. I was tired. The weather had come back up to a decent temperature and so I'd played winter golf early that morning with the Jug Hunters. My golf game hadn't been much, but I'd gained an admired skill and prowess with the bottle on the nineteenth hole from my intense legislative exposure. Practice, I supposed. I had my golfing companions swallowing hard to keep pace, but they were equal to my efforts.

I tried Judy's number again, but there still wasn't any answer. I wasn't much worried. Judy had numerous relatives in and around Capitol City. She went now and then with her son to visit them, usually on weekends. I assumed she was there.

When it was time I took the elevator. As I completed the death-defying trip, two state policemen watched me carefully as I alighted at the lobby floor. I could almost smell tension.

The senator was waiting for me in the lobby. So was Captain Carlson. They were in deep conversation. I went on up to where they were talking.

The senator said: "You're going to have to get your crystal set in the Plymouth fixed, Donald. We've missed the big news." He watched me with eyes in which I read minor dismay. "It seems that a group representing themselves as desirous of the passage of the anti-pollution bill have kidnaped one of your colleagues. The captain was just showing me a copy of the ransom note. All of the newspapers, television and radio stations received them a little while ago."

"Who got kidnaped?" I asked.

Captain Carlson looked carefully at the note. "A Representative Olean . . . Fred Olean."

"Jesus," I said. "That ought to turn things on real hard."

"They say in the note that they'll kill him if the bill isn't passed by tomorrow," Carlson said.

"That's stupid," I said. "What's passed today can be repealed the day thereafter. Most of those kids who've been marching around the Statehouse know that."

Carlson sighed. "They've got an answer for that, too. If the bill is repealed after it's passed they claim they'll kill five members of the house in reprisal." He watched me. "Maybe one of those far-out groups who've been sniping and looting and cooking nitro got Olean."

I shook my head, unable to reason. "How and when did they get him?"

He shrugged. "No one really knows. No one knew he was gone until the letters came. We've been trying to locate him ever since without any results. Last time he was seen was Friday night when he was on the town with you."

"We went to George's Rendezvous," I explained. "He was my contact out there that I told you about. I left him when we arrived back here at the hotel."

"Well, whoever it was must have taken him soon thereafter," Carlson commented. "Didn't he go home on weekends?"

"Not normally."

"He's married, isn't he?"

I shook my head. "His wife got killed in an auto accident

about five years back. His kids are grown and on their own—emancipated."

"We couldn't get an answer at his home telephone," he said. "I guess that's why." He watched me. "What are you going to do?"

"First of all I'm going to have some food. Then I'm going to talk to some of my constituents."

"Students?" he asked, interested.

I nodded.

"Am I allowed to go?" the senator asked.

"Only for food. I'm buying yours and Captain Carlson's if he cares to join us. Tomorrow you'll get hooked firmly on a state breast, Senator. After that, all is on you. Caviar and pheasant under glass for lunch. Something heavier and more exotic for dinner."

He nodded. "You've been here too long, Donald."

Five blocks away from the Statehouse, in a black depressed area, the various aboveground student organizations had rented a shabby old house for their headquarters.

I'd been there for the opening of the house and the party thereafter. Late in the party I'd even been invited to turn on and politely declined. I'd then been told indignantly by the inviter that Mary Jane is a lot less harmful to you than alcohol. Someone had shushed him and led him away and I'd never seen him again. He'd been too young, under our state laws, to drink anyhow, so how could he know? He had, however, been old enough to fight.

I had much wine that day and night and made a short speech, which was politely applauded. Some of the kids had looked right through me though and sometimes I'd felt like a prostitute in church. I was overage for the crowd. You can be overage and *be there*, but you have to have a special ticket to qualify and I didn't own the ticket. I wore my hair only middling long, I'd never been busted, never made the papers by representing some group supposedly oppressed by the powers, wasn't really rabid about my dislike of war, and sort of in favor of our form of government.

But I owed the kids. They'd supported me. I'd been preferable to eight-term Charlie, my fall opponent, so I'd had grudging support and let's forget the primary.

They'd gone door to door for me, worked the polls on Election Day giving out my cards, and maybe even gained me as many votes as I'd lost by having their support. These days having the kids for you is a sort of dubious gift. When they favor you, you can bet that the hard-hat vote will go the other way, the bigot vote is forever lost, and some of the short hairs will view you with a biased eye. As to that loss, my reaction was about like Coger Rock's, prosecutor in Bington. He told me once, after an election, and I digested it, that he didn't want to be universally loved. There were, said Coger, a lot of sons of bitches around that he'd really prefer to have mad at him all of the time.

It was dark outside, so I took a cab. Capitol City is fairly quiet at night, but a pedestrian any more is subject to many things besides robbery and mugging. Even the gendarmes don't trust a walker. We live in a period of automatic pedestrian distrust. The only safe place to walk in Capitol City is from one bar to the next in the downtown district. The police view people who do that as mere conventiongoers and not potential troublemakers.

No one was guarding the door outside. I went on inside the building. Two girls looked me over from the rear of a hall. They were handsome and wore very short skirts. They were piling up leaflets near a naked electric light. What with the light and the length of their skirts and the bending up

93

and down to pile up the leaflets I was fairly, if not intimately, acquainted with both girls by the time I reached their end of the hall.

Some of the kids they grow these days are almost hauntingly beautiful. It's as if nature, sensing that this might be the final generation (assuming we've managed to screw it up good enough to make the difference), wants to show us just how things might have been if the wheel had kept turning. The two girls I watched were examples of that. One of them was black and one of them was white and they were both memorable.

I said: "I'm Don Robak. I'd like to talk to Harlan Hill if I could."

One of the girls, the black one, nodded coolly at me. "We know who you are, Representative Robak." She looked warningly at the other girl and then back at me. "You wait right here," she said to me. She looked at the other girl. "Carol, now you watch him. Don't touch him. Just watch. I'll go see if Harlan wants to talk to him." She turned and her skirt flipped insolently at me and she was gone up the stairs in a flash of legs and all.

The other girl smiled and went back to piling up leaflets. She eyed me carefully, not with anger, but not saying anything. She had long, lovely legs. I think she was aware of it. So was I.

I said: "I don't mind if you touch." She smiled a little more, but she didn't touch me.

From the top of the steps the black girl called. Her voice was severe. "You can come on up now. You send him on up, Carol."

I went up the steps.

Harlan Hill is a middling-sized black man. He appears to be about seventeen years old and is actually twenty-four. He's a Vietnam veteran having gone in as a private and come out a bemedaled first lieutenant, which isn't easy for anyone, and I guess is tougher if you're black. He's a very bright boy, but sometimes I doubt his stability. Now he's president of the student body organization down at the state university in Bington. Lots of blacks get elected presidents of student body organizations these days. Some deserve it.

If Harlan doesn't breed trust in you, still he is impressive. In the campaign I once saw some kind of bigot, who was half again Harlan's size, try him on to see if he could find a fit. The fight was short and deadly. The large guy wound up in a hospital and Harlan failed to work up a good sweat.

I thought the fight could have been avoided. The bigot was mostly mouth and deserved someone ignoring him. Harlan disagreed.

I saw Joe Metzco around Harlan once and Metzco treated him gingerly and with real respect. That impressed me because Harlan surely is the embodiment of all that far-winger Metzco hates.

Now Harlan was here in Capitol City running the students' protest movement. I'd seen him that one day I'd been to the dedication of this headquarters and I'd talked several times on the phone to him. Things went okay, but both of us worked at it.

We aren't real friends. He doesn't want any white, real friends my age. I think he sort of hates me, but hides it well.

He was sitting at an old desk in a big, high-ceilinged room. He had on loafers without socks, a short-sleeved shirt and summer walking shorts, although the house temperature seemed about fifty to me.

Other desks were in the room, some of them occupied. I'd heard the tentative tap-tap of typewriters as I came up the steps, but when I was inside the room all sound died and

95

eyes watched me. I thought they were waiting for something wrong to happen. With no luck, it probably would.

"Hello, Harlan," I said.

He nodded. "Representative Robak," he murmured carefully. He looked around the room playing to his captive audience: "Look under the beds if you want. We don't have him. If any of our people even know about it the word hasn't gotten here yet. And we've checked about everyone."

"I want you to find him," I said softly.

He looked a little surprised. "I just told you we're not responsible for taking him." He inspected me as if I had bagworms. "If I find out that any of our people have him then I assure you he'll be released immediately. That's the best I can do for you, Mr. Representative."

I shook my head. "That is not enough. I want you to put your kids at finding him. I want to be able to say they found him when no one else could do the job."

He smiled coldly. "Go away. Help the police look for him. You'll do more good there."

"Think about it a little bit, Harlan. Tomorrow we'll suspend the rules and pass anti-pollution in both houses and the governor will sign it." I looked at his cool, black face. "Are you for the bill?" I asked.

"Mildly. One or two of the groups are really for it."

"And after Olean makes it back, despite all threats, what do you think will happen to it?"

"They'll repeal it," he said simply.

"Sure. And I'll tell you what else they'll do. They'll be angry. They'll pass your tuition rise, if it hits the floor.

"We have some other steps should they do that," he said.

"Good old fire and revolution. Snipers on the rooftops and down with the fuzz. That may bring you more change than you're ready for, Harlan."

96

He smiled his cool smile. "There are other, peaceful ways. We'll try those first." He nodded, almost to himself. "We could just refuse to pay the raise, start in attending classes, make them do something to stop us."

"Think about it my way, Harlan. There's a chance that they may be mad enough over there to just close the whole business down for a time, not appropriate any money to run the universities. Maybe that's what whoever took Olean really wants."

He shrugged. "And so?"

I felt deflated. "And so nothing. I'm just telling you the way it might be if Olean isn't found tonight. I'm telling you that there are numerous people who don't really want him found."

"The police . . ." he began.

"I don't believe the Capitol City police are taking much interest in the matter. The only police I saw around the Blue Hotel were the state boys. I didn't see one Capitol City cop."

"We see them," he said. "Usually, in the daytime, there's never less than a squad around here. They're not in uniform, but they're obviously cops. They've worked on the telephone line outside so many times they've driven Bell stock up. They live inside the manholes in the street out there, they drive almost all of the trucks that park in front. They even carry the mail in this block. They've come in with search warrants four times since we've been up here. Once we caught one of them trying to plant some stuff we figure was maybe heroin underneath the lid of the garbage pail when they picked up the garbage." He grinned without humor. "We've got a pretty good bond fund. They bust us, we make bond. They haven't got guts enough to try us in a real court. All we've seen so far are police-type judges."

I nodded. "But it looks good for them in the newspapers.

They're giving this town what it wants when they harass you." I inspected the room. I'd noticed once or twice out of the corner of my eye that the black girl who'd brought me in was nodding now and then when I said something. I was encouraged a little by it.

"I doubt if your bond fund will hold up for long if they pick up a bunch of you for kidnaping," I said. "Even if they set bond."

"We didn't take him," he said again, exasperation in his voice.

"I believe you," I said. "I may be the only one who ever does believe you. If Olean isn't back by morning then remember that I believed you. I'm sure that'll solve all your problems." I got up and moved toward the door. "If you do find him and need any help call me at the Blue Hotel." I sighed, realizing how tired I was. "I'm going back there and try to sleep."

No one said anything or nodded. I went to the door and on out. Downstairs I had the remaining miniskirted girl call me a cab, although I really hated to leave her.

I slept finally and dreamed a little and was awakened in the early morning by someone banging hard on my door. I got up grumpily, hand hunted for the light switch on the bedside table and finally found it.

My shoulder hurt a little and I remembered that I'd been dreaming about that long ago day when I'd raised up at the wrong time and been hemstitched by a patient, loving machine gunner. Now all that was left were the two scars, somewhat larger in the rear than they were in front. I can tell sometimes when the weather is going to change. A few inches farther in and I doubt if I'd had to worry about weather changes.

"Who is it?" I asked.

From the other side of the door a deep voice said: "Uncle Tom."

I recognized the voice and unbolted things and threw the door open.

Fred Olean stood there. He was rumpled and unshaven. His suit jacket was torn at the left cuff. He looked tired, but not really too bad. He grinned at me and I banged him on the back, very glad to see him.

"Careful with the merchandise," he said. "A man told me I should check in here before I went to bed."

"Who's that?"

"A little black boy named Harlan Hall," he said, nodding. "Three of his kids came busting into this place where I was tied up. They untied me and called him and he came. Then they brought me back to the hotel here." He inspected his watch. "That was about an hour ago. I've been talking to policemen since. They just turned me loose."

"Who had you, Fred?"

He shook his head. "I don't know, Don. You and I came back from George's place. They were in my room. They must have unscrewed a light, you know the one you turn on from the door. It didn't go on when I tried. I think a couple of them held me and another one gave me a shot. There may have been more than that involved." He grinned. "I'm such a tiger, you know. Anyway they held something over my mouth so I couldn't yell and gave me a shot. I could feel the sting of it. When I woke up I was tied down and gagged and blindfolded. Once I thought they were gone and I tried to work my way loose and someone must have been watching me. I got clonked pretty good on the head and I was told to cut it out. Later, when I didn't hear anything, I tried again, but I wasn't doing much good. I think whoever had me heard those kids coming—they were going house to house and room to room almost. I was getting kind of hungry and pretty thirsty when those kids came in." He shook his head. "The ones who got me—they had me hid in an abandoned house that's due to be torn down for redevelopment. It's only a few blocks from where those kids have their headquarters. I was all wrapped up nice. Harlan said his kids didn't do it. He wanted me to tell you that again." He shrugged. "I believe him."

"You don't sound like you're sure," I said. "I imagine if his kids had taken you they wouldn't have hidden you out within yelling distance of their headquarters. They're not that dumb. But it could have been other kids."

He tapped his brow, as if trying to remember. "One more thing. I was under when they were taking me to that place, but once I came up out of it and knew I was in a car, and I could hear them talking. I keep trying to remember what they were saying, but nothing comes." He stopped for a moment and considered. "They didn't sound like college kids."

"How do you mean?" I asked.

"There's a way people talk. The ones who had me—well they didn't talk like college kids."

"Did you tell the police that?"

He nodded. "I told your friend, Captain Carlson. He didn't pay much attention." He knuckled his eyes. "I'm dead on my feet."

I pointed at my bed. "Be smart and sleep right there. I'll bet every reporter in the state is trying to locate you now."

He nodded. "Good idea. That reminds me." He reached inside his coat pocket and came out with a copy of the early edition of the Capitol City *Enquirer* and handed it to me. "Captain Carlson gave that to me for you."

The headline was bold and ran the full top of the front page. LEGISLATOR KIDNAPED, it screamed.

The story below theorized strongly that the kidnaping had probably been carried out by the gang of student activists who'd terrorized the city during the legislative session.

There was also a cartoon in the middle of the front page. It showed Polsen, Chapell and myself hunting clues near-sightedly, wearing Sherlock hats and carrying magnifying glasses. There wasn't anything where we were looking, but in the background, students dismantled the Statehouse. Our caricatures were labeled so there'd be no doubt. We looked very stupid and the students appeared very sly. The caption below the cartoon read: *Modern Criminal Investigation Finds the General Assembly.*

There was a short feature story about the committee. It made us look like a bunch of clods setting out to muddy the waters so that Sloan's murderer(s), if any, would never be found. I was described in the article as a small-town attorney with no previous legislative experience. The article made it appear that I had little going for me, which was true I supposed. Polsen and Chapell were a little tougher for the writer, but he glossed them over quickly and then took great glee in going immediately to the fact that I'd been the last person who'd seen Fred Olean before his kidnaping. That, and the fact that I represented the dissident kids from Bington who were mocking the law, were the main points of the article.

"It's libelous, isn't it?" Fred asked hopefully when I was done and had given him back the paper.

"I don't really know," I said. "Maybe it is. George Chapell might want to sue them. He belongs to the party the newspaper is supposed to identify with and he might want to tap them. I wouldn't want to be in the same courtroom with them myself. Too close. Surely to God they'd shake and you'd get that crap all over you."

He looked at me, tired and not really comprehending.

I smiled. "Take that bed and sleep. After you get some sleep you'll understand why I said that. I'll hang the DO NOT DISTURB sign on the door. And I'll call you like say about three o'clock this afternoon. Double-lock the door after me and don't answer it."

He nodded and yawned. "Thanks, Don," he said. "That Harlan Hill said I maybe ought to thank you." He grinned at me. "Until those kids got me out of that room and he saw me, I don't think he knew I was black. The ones who were doing the looking knew, but he didn't."

I shook my head. "He probably still doesn't believe it. You're a white in black make-up to him. You're a success. You want to live in the world, not die in it. Someday, hopefully, Harlan will want that also, but not now. He's not so very far away from the nitro cookers. The only thing that was in his eyes and in his head last night when I talked to him was indifference. He looked for you to further his own cause, not because it was right. Your disappearance could have hurt him, blocked what he wanted."

Olean smiled at me. "Little black sheep," he said and made no further amplification. He sat down on the bed and removed his shoes.

"Sleep tight," I said. "And don't forget the door. I'll tell them downstairs not to ring the room."

"Segregate me," he said sleepily.

Outside I waited until I heard him lock the door. I put the DO NOT DISTURB sign on the outer doorknob. Downstairs in the Blue I told them that my old-maid aunt was in the room and wanted no phone calls until three o'clock.

CHAPTER IX

RULE 21. *Members of the legislature shall not use foul language. . . .*

The first gentleman I met when I got to the Statehouse after breakfast was a reporter I didn't know, but who'd been pointed out to me before. The representative who'd identified him for me had said impressively: "That's Jack Brofile. He's the hatchetman for the Capitol City *Enquirer*." And so he was.

He shoved his press card in my face. "I'm Jack Brofile," he said. He was a long, thin man, not young.

"How nice for you," I said and kept walking.

He kept up with me. "I'd like to ask you some questions."

I stopped. "Why?" I asked. "I read your paper this morning. They already have the answers. You're not going to print anything in that rag that doesn't fit in your editorial line." I smiled at him. "Why bother with facts?"

He went right on, ignoring what I said: "About this committee investigating the death of Sloan Link. I hear that you know who killed Link. That's the word I'm getting—that you know."

I considered it. "No comment," I said.

"I'm informed he was taking money for something and that a group of legislators found out he was taking. I hear they plotted his death."

That sort of story belonged in the Capitol City paper. "No comment," I said, concealing amusement.

"Have you any comment on anything, Representative Robak?" he asked sarcastically.

"No comment," I said, without changing expression.

The second guy who approached me was T. J. Toy. There was a smile on his face, triumph in his eyes.

"You going to have a Judiciary Committee meeting today?" he asked.

I smiled just a little. "I doubt it, T.J." I shook my head. "I guess we ought to wait a bit until things calm down. In the interest of fair play," I added.

My answer seemed unexpected. He watched me with unconcealed hate in his eyes. "Things aren't going to calm down as long as there's riotous mobs in the streets and lawlessness is tolerated," he said darkly.

"You sound as if you've been giving careful attention to the editorial page of the Capitol City *Enquirer*," I said mildly.

He shook his head, ignoring my words. "It's getting late in the session. I think the people of this state have a right to know what bills are going to come out of your committee, Robak." He gave me his best hard look. "That way my interested parties can have their say with the individual legislators."

I was getting a little angry, but I concealed it with another small smile. I said: "One bill you can bet will come out recommended for passage is anti-pollution, Mr. Toy. But it won't come out today. No, sir. It *will* come out when an investigation has been made into who kidnaped Representative Olean and why he was taken. So far Olean says it probably wasn't college kids who took him. College kids are the ones who found him, after being requested to look."

"They *should* know," he said. "Maybe you should too. I understand you went to see them late last night."

"To ask them to look," I said reasonably, feeling my insides redden more. "And they found him. I want the word to spread on that. I want the police to look for the men who had Olean. There's plenty of time in this session for the passage of any bill or for its defeat. You'll have to wait."

"I demand you meet today," he said. "If you don't comply with this reasonable request I'm going to turn my dogs loose on you, Robak. My people will drive you and the rest of this legislature crazy attempting to explain why they're not getting a fair shake." He smiled coldly. "They'll send you over the edge, Robak. You couldn't even be elected a notary public after they get through with you."

"I am frightened to death," I said carefully.

"You'd better be," he said pompously, taking my words at face value.

I lost whatever remaining temper I possessed. Carefully, in cogent language, I explained to him what his demand meant to me and what value it had. I was explicit. When I was done his face was white. He made no attempt to take advantage of any of the illegal or immoral courses of action I pointed out as available to him. Instead, he turned his back and stormed away.

And there went my chances with the go-go girls. There went a source of free liquor, paid-up hotel bills, nights on the town. I sighed and figuratively tightened my belt.

T.J. didn't like me any more.

I went on into the legislative chamber and hung my coat. I went to my seat and was accosted by several members of the Judiciary Committee. Each wanted to know when the meeting was supposed to be held. Each, upon careful prodding, could relate the information that there was to be a meeting back to T.J. or someone T.J. could easily have told.

So I gave vague answers. I cited the fact that Olean was back, added that he didn't believe student activists had kidnaped him, mentioned darkly that the state police were interested in the matter.

There was no need for haste. Maybe we'd meet tomorrow, maybe later, I said.

The word spread around the floor. I got some curious glances, but I also got relief.

Soon after, a tiny, excited (probably because he was out of school) page hurried up to my seat with a note. I opened it and discovered that Speaker McGuire desired me to come to his office for an important conference—*immediately*.

I walked out through the fishbowl, which is the glassed area behind the chamber where crowds can watch. I understand the glass is bulletproof, which shows someone was thinking. Out there a crowd suspiciously watched the legislative floor. Many of the watchers were little old ladies with determined faces, flourishing black umbrellas. Some of them were clenching hard at a piece of legislation, studying it. I wondered if they were T.J.'s troops, come quickly after me, and then I remembered. Today the house was to vote on the newest obscenity bill in a long line thereof. The watchers were undoubtedly members of that sterling organization, the Ladies for Decent Literature. I'd heard they came almost every year. The Supreme Court keeps knocking down my state's obscenity laws and each legislature dutifully passes a new one, so that the ladies with black umbrellas (and white tennis shoes) can live happily. I thought privately that some of the watchers might be alarmed at parts of the Bible, if unidentified and read aloud.

Speaker McGuire had his office down the corridor that flanked the legislative chamber. Inside there was room enough for his secretary in an anteroom and then a fairly large adjoining office for himself.

Outside today a state policeman watched me nervously as I tapped at the door and was only mildly reassured when I was readily admitted.

McGuire had his shoes off and his feet, in great hairy socks, were propped on his desk. A bottle of Chivas Regal was also on the desk along with an ice container, a bottle of soda and some extra glasses on a tray. McGuire was toying with a glass.

In the far corner of the room, drinkless, at attention, sat Captain Carlson. He nodded at me.

McGuire pointed lazily at the scotch. "Pour yourself a belt, Robak."

I took a clue from Carlson and shook my head. "I can't take it this early in the morning," I said. I smiled regretfully at him. "I guess I just don't have your constitution, Mr. Speaker."

He frowned, but not at me. "Doctor says my blood pressure is too damned high. Damned fool told me to give up drinking for a year. Maybe I will sometime—year after next." He waved fairly affably at a chair. "Sit down. Sit down!" he ordered.

I sat. I looked over at Carlson, but nothing passed across his face.

McGuire leaned forward. "Carlson tells me he's assigned extra men to watch the legislative floors and the various downtown hotels. He also thinks they may have a line on the people who got Olean."

"How's that?" I asked, turning to Carlson.

"Got a description of the people who'd been living in that house. We may even have a tentative identification of one of them from our mug books. We've got a pick-up out on the 'possible' on a preliminary charge of kidnaping, which will be big bond or no bond. He's a pro, Representative Robak. If he's the one then your kids had nothing to do with it."

McGuire cut in. "Captain Carlson also said you asked him to check on T. J. Toy. Did you do that, Representative Robak?"

I nodded. "I guess I did. He'd been socializing with Link the night that Link wound up out the window. He's also been notoriously pushy about the anti-pollution matter, which Link proposed. He may have been the person who had the pushing done. He may also have been the one who had Olean taken." I watched him, trying to read something in his eyes. Nothing was apparent. "I thought he ought to be checked out."

He nodded. "In the checking, Captain Carlson has found that Mr. Toy probably isn't eligible to be a lobbyist in this state." He leaned forward and put his feet down. "Mr. Toy was convicted of a felony in a nearby state about seven years back. Persons who've been convicted of a felony and who haven't received a pardon aren't allowed to practice lobbying in this state." He inspected me with some care. "We don't have all of the word about it yet. Captain Carlson and I were trying to determine what we should do about it with the information we now hold. We thought you should be in on the discussion."

"Thank you," I said. I hesitated and added: "And perhaps Representatives Polsen and Chapell? Shouldn't they be here also?"

"I'll leave it up to you to report back what you desire," McGuire said brusquely. "Captain Carlson told me that you were the one who was actually working with the state people, not Polsen or Chapell."

"All right," I said. I turned to Carlson. "What was T.J. convicted of?"

"Manslaughter," Carlson said. "I don't have any of the details about the case. I don't even know whether it was 'vol' or 'invol'. All I have is the fact that he was convicted of manslaughter. Way I got it is by checking him back. He gave some past addresses when he got his lobbyist's permit. One of those addresses was out of state, a place he'd worked. I called. It was a factory. He worked there for a year before he came into this state. On his application he showed the conviction. On his application here in this state for a lobbying permit he didn't show it."

"Did he do any time?"

He shook his head. "I don't know. I've got a call in to all three of the penal institutions in that state. He might be a parole violator, he might not. Anyway he falsified his application here when he applied as a lobbyist." He watched me with thoughtful eyes. "What with the Link matter still unresolved and the Olean kidnaping, I thought perhaps we'd put him under surveillance and hold up doing anything until we get full information," he ended suggestively. "The offense here is a misdemeanor."

I thought about it. Even without primary evidence in the Link matter I knew that if T. J. Toy was arrested as an offender under our statutes or removed from the state as a parole violator, he would be, from that time on, the newspapers' probable murderer of Sloan Link. I owed him no favors and picking him up would even be beneficial to me. I could claim discovery of him by my request to check him out. It was sort of an attractive way to wash stained linen, dispose of a perplexing matter.

I watched Carlson. "Do you want to wait for a while?"

"With him under surveillance, I'd like to," he said. "All that we have now is the misdemeanor thing and the fact that he just might be a parole violator. If we watch him maybe we can tie him to the kidnap of Representative Olean, maybe even to the Link murder." His voice slowed. "There could be some danger in it, I suppose."

I nodded. That was true. I was in the way on anti-pollution. The danger was mine and I felt uncomfortable thinking about it. But even if T.J. was picked up he'd make bond and the danger could still be there. I supposed I was better off just waiting, knowing that T.J. was being watched.

"I suppose," I said reluctantly, "that picking up T.J. one day is as good as another, so I'll go along with the wait."

We all nodded at each other and the bargain was made.

Captain Carlson got up. "We've also tried to run down the prints on that crank letter, but nothing's come back yet." He shook his head. "Don't expect anything on it, Representative Robak. I think we're looking the right way on T. J. Toy. He's our man. Trouble will be in proving it."

I was reminded by his statement. "How about the other letter?" I asked.

He shrugged. "An advertisement." He nodded at Speaker McGuire and shook hands with me. "Thank you both for your help," he said and went out the door.

McGuire waited politely for me to leave, but I sat back down.

"Might I ask the Speaker a few things that might be of help?"

He nodded curtly. "Go ahead."

"I've heard that you and Representative Link had an argument on the night he was killed. What was it about?"

He smiled coolly. "Link and I have been arguing and fighting with each other for close to twenty years. As you may have heard I have at least the desire for a higher office. That night I went up to the Finance rooms. Link was there and he was in one of his rough, jovial moods. I wasn't. He called me the 'outstanding consumers' candidate.' I figured he was picking at me again for being fat and it hit me very wrong. So we argued. It didn't mean a thing. We even had some drinks later on that evening together. Everything was okay. Earlier was just a bad moment."

"That later time—was that when you were with T. J. Toy out at George's Rendezvous?"

He nodded. "A bunch of us. Only thing I remember out of the way was one of your kids picking at Link. The club people ran the kid off." He shook his head, remembering. "We were fairly peaceful. Someone was trying to get Polsen to explain the cross-state power bill he wants and Chapell was doing some pretty forceful kidding with Link. All about how anti-pollution would ruin Link's mix so that Maker's Mark would never taste the same to him again." He grinned.

"I've heard a bit about cross-state power," I said, "but I'm still sort of uninformed. What is it and why is it so hot?"

He considered me, frowning at my ignorance. "It's a bill that would allow a plant doing business and located outside this state to erect power transmission lines into this state and compete in the power market."

I nodded, beginning to see.

He went on: "If a power company in another state could raid large users they could sell power very cheaply. The power companies here have to take care of all users. Chapell and Polsen think it would be good for competition." He shrugged. "The state people are dead against it. I doubt there is a real 'right' to it. It's just whose ox is being gored."

"Is there a lot of money involved?"

His eyes flickered. "Could be. The in-state boys have an ex-governor hired to lobby against it. The outers have a whole team around. Soft sell so far, but it will get warmer." He nodded thoughtfully at me.

I nodded back and returned to the subject.

"Did you see Link again after leaving George's Rendezvous?"

He shook his head carefully and I couldn't read his eyes.

"T.J. was pushing the booze hard. I'd had enough. I went on back to the Blue and to bed. I don't know any way to prove to you that I didn't get up later and go to Link's room and shove him out his window. You'll just have to take my word for it or refuse to take my word for it." He watched me, his face graven. "The only thing is that I plan to be a candidate for U. S. Senator. God help you if you mess that up. I had me a chunk of bad publicity once. I'm telling you that I'll protect myself and throw anyone away who tries to slip me more." His eyes were cold and far away, remembering. "I lost three thousand votes off my majority that year. Got back in the house by the skin of my teeth." He shook his head. "I hadn't done anything wrong, but I put someone in a position where he could make it look like I'd done wrong. It taught me to protect myself at all times. So I'll say to you again: God help you if you mess me up."

I wondered if it could have been God help Link, too, but I only smiled and nodded. "Thank you for the information, Mr. Speaker. Thanks also for asking me in on the T. J. Toy matter."

We shook hands. His hand was large and powerful. He seemed strong enough.

"I still don't like those kids of yours, Robak," he said, and I thought he was just searching around for something to say and that was the first thing that came.

"They aren't my kids, Mr. Speaker. They come from all over this state. Some are from outside this state. I just have them down in Bington with me for a little while. You'll get back your county's share in the summertime and upon graduation."

He nodded and I could see that the idea caused him some pain.

"All right," he said, accepting it a little. He went further in his effort to be congenial. "See you at the governor's reception tonight?" he asked.

I nodded. I'd forgotten again about the governor's party, but I was willing to wager that Judy hadn't. I was glad he'd reminded me. I'm afraid I have a poor memory for formal things like ties and shoes and mix with whiskey.

Back on the legislative floor I sweated the day out. T. J. Toy was as good as his word. Pages kept bringing me insulting telegrams. Western Union must have moved up a point or two in the market. I had a large waste can under my desk. I kept opening the telegrams and looking at the signatures and then depositing the telegrams there. By late afternoon I'd about filled it. Other legislators got pressure telegrams also, but I was by far the favorite target.

A few of the telegrams were from Bington residents. One was from a man who ran a small manufacturing plant outside the town. He was a nice, sharp fellow and I'd represented him once or twice in routine legal matters. It was apparent that he began by sending the T.J.-requested canned message, for his telegram began like most of the others.

It read: "Release H.B. 1732 for vote. Let us be heard." But then he went further. "That's what I got told to wire you, Don." Then: "What's H.B. 1732?"

I also got a lot of long-distance telephone calls, but I

quickly notified the operator that I wasn't going to take any from outside Mojeff County, my own bailiwick. I took only messages on the others. All day long patient pages kept bringing me notes to call operator seven in South Vernon or operator twelve in West Bend.

The anti-pornography bill passed without a dissenting vote. I heard one representative complain about it later. He said that a group of the aging ladies had attempted to brain him in the hallway when he explained the criminal penalty on the bill was only five years. He referred to his attackers as "the bent-umbrella brigade."

"Not enough," they screamed and swung. He found refuge in a men's room, where they failed to follow.

When the house broke session for the day, I walked down several flights of steps bearing my basketful of telegrams.

The parking attendant for the Statehouse lot knew T. J. Toy's car and courteously described it for me. I marched along rows of cars parked in the lot and finally found it, unlocked.

I scattered the telegrams over T.J.'s rich auto interior. At the entrance to the lot an armed state policeman watched me curiously as I handfuled some here and some there. He waved gaily at me when I was done, figuring if that was what I wanted to do with my telegrams that was okay with him. I waved back.

•

CHAPTER X

RULE 24. *Members shall offer to the governor all respects due his office.*

At eight that night, via cab, Judy and I approached the governor's mansion. As we drew near, the cabbie sighed and his meter clicked and I could see a long line of traffic going up the narrow drive.

I looked at Judy and she nodded.

"Let us out here, driver."

We got out into a night that was cold but fair and equipped with a huge winter moon. Up the drive state police officers were trying to keep traffic moving. What little space there was available for easy parking was already filled and they were parking the overflow now on the grass and were hampered by trees and bushes.

Judy had swayed audibly between dresses and finally settled upon a little black cocktail outfit. She'd then covered it with a rich fur, a remnant of her marriage. She held my hand tightly and a nervous pulse raced in her throat, but her eyes were bright and inquisitive.

I'd asked my law partner, Senator Adams, to ride with us,

but he'd quickly found old cronies from his own legislative days and had decided to ride out with them.

The front of the mansion was ablaze with lights. I was uncomfortable in my formal clothes and tried to remember the last time I'd worn them. If my memory of the date was correct I hoped nothing had turned green.

A busy maid took our coats and stroked Judy's with admiration. She traded me a metal tag for them and we went on.

Governor Bratewell and his wife headed a reception line made up of the top state officials and wives. We pursued our way down it smiling and shaking limp hands.

Bratewell himself leaned forward and whispered to me: "There's better stuff in the kitchen for those in need." His wife watched him and tried not to disapprove too much.

To the left, in a faded ballroom, a band played unenthusiastic music to a sparse crowd of dancers. In the large room to the right there was an austere line of punch bowls sitting perfumed and poisonously green. Elegantly dressed people stood near the punch bowls. Here and there polite little conversation groups had formed. I got Judy and me two cups of punch plus a small cookie for her. I also filched her an extra paper napkin she could slip into her purse for a souvenir. I held my own punch carefully, afraid to taste it. A client, who drank a bit, once told me you could get accustomed to that soft stuff and then where were you?

"Dance?" I asked resignedly.

But surprisingly she shook her head, more intent upon the sights and sounds around her.

I spied Speaker McGuire in the hall and I had trouble for a moment recognizing the beautifully dressed woman with upswept hair that he was ponderously escorting. It was Link's ex-girl friend, Gertrude May. They came on into the room and McGuire parked Gertrude with us while he went for punch and after I'd made the introductions.

The girls cackled brightly together; and I inspected the crowd.

George Chapell was in evidence, equipped with a wife who clutched tightly at his arm. She was wearing a gown and a tiara. Her tightly cinched figure plowed here and there, a battleship among mini-vessels.

My partner, Senator Adams, had told me that once she'd owned a set of warms for Sloan Link. I wanted to ask her about that, though I doubted I'd get much out of her. I waited patiently, figuring the governor had told Chapell about the kitchen source also, swallowing hard and trying to outlast him. Already, in my thirst, it seemed to me that the room had more female occupants than male.

Speaker McGuire was taking his time about returning with the punch. Gertrude May watched the dancers longingly. I ignored her until Judy punched me lightly in the ribs.

"Uh—would you like to dance, Gertrude?" I asked gallantly.

Both women beamed. Gertrude attached herself to an arm and I escorted her into the ballroom. When we were on the dance floor she draped herself on and near me and we danced after a fashion.

"Is that your girl?" she asked.

I nodded. I could see Judy watching us from the other room. She wasn't beaming now. Gertrude hunched everything a little closer.

"Little young for you, isn't she?" she asked severely.

"She's older than she looks," I answered mildly.

"I suppose it isn't any of my business anyway," she said, trying to appear forlorn about it all.

I thought about it. "I'm glad you're interested," I said. "How about you and me for tomorrow? A drink or three when I get done?"

She brightened. "I'll wait for you at the office." She hesitated in midstep. "What about little Miss what's-her-name?" I assumed she meant Judy.

"I'll do the worrying about that," I said. "We aren't married." I hoped that Judy would forgive me. I did need to talk to Gertrude about Sloan Link. She'd probably known Sloan as well as he'd ever been known and there were still things about Sloan that I didn't know. Maybe something she knew could help me.

The dance finally finished and she removed herself from me bit by bit. We went on back into the "punch" room where Speaker McGuire stood sweating and gingerly holding two glasses of punch. He was talking to Judy and she was watching me with a little heat in her eyes.

McGuire gave one of the glasses of punch to Gertrude, looked at the other doubtfully, then gulped it down. He coughed twice and I watched him expectantly, but nothing bad happened. Gertrude winked at me and they wandered on. I didn't try to find my own punch.

Judy said coldly: "I only wanted you to dance with her, Don. I didn't want you to make love to her right in the middle of the dance floor. I was mortified. She was all over you."

"She's Link's ex-girl friend," I said placatingly. "I guess she's harmless. I need to talk to her again. I'm going to have to buy her some drinks tomorrow when I get done with things."

She sighed and almost visibly decided against anger. "Wear enough clothes for protection," she said. "Maybe I should loan you one of my girdles."

I started to say that I had my doubts that I could get into her girdle, but I figured she'd take it amiss as an ambiguous remark. Regretfully, I let it pass.

Out of the corner of my eye I saw George Chapell, sans wife, heading for what I assumed was the bar in the kitchen. I looked around for his formidable wife and saw her standing alone in a corner of the room.

There's a natural instinct among partygoers to try to include an "alone," make the lonely one a part of the festivities. I admitted to myself that Mrs. Chapell didn't strike that chord in me, but I wanted to talk to her so I pretended the feeling.

"Let's go over and talk to Mrs. Chapell," I said to Judy. "She's all alone over there. I guess her husband's gone to the kitchen."

She nodded and I took her hand and we walked on over to Mrs. Chapell. She watched our coming with challenging eyes that I refused to let daunt me.

I introduced myself and Judy in case she'd forgotten who I was.

"I know your husband very well," I said, trying to make conversation.

She seemed uncomfortable about something and I figured she didn't like to be in the same corner with Judy, didn't like the obvious comparison.

"He's such a busy, busy man," she said in her high voice. "All of those people over there who depend on him, who need him. All of those decisions he has to make."

I waited and a silence came.

Mrs. Chapell was watching Judy. "That's such a nice frock, dear," she said. "Did you make it yourself?"

Judy flushed a little. "No," she said shortly and then named a famous designer whose name sounded a bit obscene.

"He made it." I thought she might say even more, but conversation stopped as the governor's wife came into the room.

"If anyone is interested I'm going to conduct a tour of this ancient, governmental castle. It will depart from the entrance hallway stairs in about two minutes," she said and beamed all around at the other ladies.

Judy turned questioningly to me.

"You go, Judy," I said. "It'll be all women. I don't think I'd fit. Besides, I have a place that I need to go."

Judy looked at Mrs. Chapell. "Mrs. Chapell?" she inquired politely.

The older woman shook her head. "Dearie," she said, in that voice that could shatter wine glasses, "I've made the tour of this house too many times already."

Judy nodded coolly and excused herself and I was left standing with Mrs. Chapell who watched me without anything showing at all in her eyes.

"Why not go to the kitchen?" she asked. "That's where all the lovely men are. I wonder if you all think we don't know what's going on, didn't get the drift of what the governor was whispering." Her laugh was so brittle that it smashed in a hundred pieces.

"I wanted to talk to you," I said.

"Whatever in the world for?"

"I understand you knew and were friendly with Sloan Link?"

"I know and knew them all," she said flatly. "Not that it means a thing, but I do know all of the dear little politicians."

"Just how well did you know Sloan Link?" I asked.

She eyed me carefully. "Certainly not nearly as well as your tone implies."

"I hear there was a time," I began, refusing to be ruffled.

"Years ago," she said. "It was a nothing, a vulnerable moment." She nodded to herself, remembering. Then she became aware of me again. "Go away, young man."

"Why not tell me about it if it meant so little and ended so long ago?" I asked.

"There's nothing to tell," she said shaking her head. "I thought I saw something in him, but it wasn't ever there. I thought I saw—greatness, ability, strength—but all I found inside him was paper. He was another fool. The world is full of them." She watched me with bitter eyes. "Like you," she said. "Now go away from me. Do your tiresome questioning elsewhere, please."

I nodded. "It was so nice of you to talk to me," I said, not without irony.

She laughed at me with real amusement in her eyes. In the laughter I could see what she'd been once and perhaps a little of why Sloan Link had once wanted her. The laughter straightened the lines around her mouth and smoothed her jowls. I could tell that once, a long time back, she'd been beautiful, with that cold, cold beauty that challenges. I thought it had challenged Link once, but that was years ago and now she was old and bitter. Life had passed her and now she fought the fact of the passing with hatred.

I walked easily away and left the laughter at my back where it trilled off into the punch bowls to become only another echo.

A smiling servant opened the kitchen door for me. The press of people inside was intense. Legislators and high state officials milled about talking and gesturing in the cramped quarters. Governors in my state have never been allowed by the public or by the newspapers who "serve" that public to have open parties where alcoholic beverages are served. That was the reason for the sham, for the whisper and the wink in the reception line.

To show there'd been planning, two professional bartenders served drinks from a bar in the far corner of the kitchen. I made my way there and got a Bourbon and water. The place smelled of cigars and human sweat and whiskey. In a far corner of the room an enthusiastic crap game had begun. Dice flashed and money went from hand to floor and back to hand again. Ed Polsen and George Chapell were both in the game. I spied Speaker McGuire, free of Gertrude, watching. My friend Fred Olean stood in the background, his eyes amused. I hadn't seen him since morning, but I'd talked briefly with him when I'd called him in my room that afternoon. I'd called to awaken him, but there really hadn't been any need. By that time an enterprising reporter had already found him.

I went over to him. "You look better," I said. "Slightly less disheveled, rested, well Bourboned and fed."

He grinned. "You fit on the last two," he said.

"How'd the press treat you?" I asked. On the phone he'd told me he'd set a news conference for the afternoon.

"Fair," he said. He frowned a little. "Except for the reporter from the Capitol City *Enquirer*. He kept wanting to know how well I knew you, when we'd met, et cetera. I got the idea that he figured you and I set the whole thing up, got me kidnaped and then released for some shadowy, nefarious purpose." He smiled. "I even showed them my suit and my head. I figured they might think I'd let myself be bopped, although it's a big bump, but that's my best suit, man, and you can't ever really fix a tear like that."

"I believe you," I said solemnly. "Now, when do I get my share of the ransom money?"

He smiled just a hair and we watched the crap game. And as I watched I got an idea. It didn't seem like too good an idea, but the more I pondered it the less bad it seemed.

In the crap game they were shooting five and sometimes ten dollars a throw, but it wasn't a big game yet, just enthusiastic.

I explained my idea to Fred and he thought it was a very bad idea.

"You're crazy, man," he said and rubbed his head. "Those guys are playing rough." He shook his head. "That was my very best suit."

I picked at him for a little while and finally he acceded.

We moved on over to the fringe of the game.

Chapell had the dice. His point was nine. "Easy nine," he said fervently.

I looked at Fred. "A hundred says he makes nine," I said to him.

He gave me a sort of surprised look and then nodded. "Even?" he asked.

"Sure," I said carelessly.

Chapell watched me narrowly. "You must think I'm going to make that point," he said, contempt in his eyes.

"Roll the dice, hot man," I said.

At a hundred dollars a throw (supposedly) I began betting Fred on the side, taking sixes and eights even, taking fives and nines even. I was, of course, overmatched by the odds.

Other legislators watched me curiously. A hundred bucks a roll was pretty good money.

Polsen, a born sharpie, tried to get in on the act the next time the point was nine. He said: "I'll take half of that," when I offered the bet, looking at Fred.

Fred shook his head. "All mine," he said.

Taking even odds on five and nine made me look like an extremely stupid crapshooter, but for a while a run of luck kept me above even. I publicly exulted while Fred glowered.

"That's two hundred I'm into you, Freddie," I called.

He nodded. "I can pay," he said savagely. "Want to double it?"

"Why not?" I asked innocently. "This is my night."

But it wasn't. The dice turned. He beat me three times running, then I won twice. He began to win consistently. We quit, as agreed, when I was down two thousand to him.

We walked away from the game arguing audibly and not too amiably about when and where I'd pay him.

When we were out of earshot I nodded at him. "Now I'm not only a curious legislator asking a lot of questions and making people mad, but I'm also a curious legislator who owes or has lost two thousand bucks."

"Don't thank me," he said, still playing the game. "Just pay me."

"How about working it out of my share of the ransom money?" I suggested.

He nodded. "They paid what my worthless hide was worth. Giving you credit for half then you still owe me nineteen hundred ninety-nine dollars."

I spied my law partner come panting through the kitchen door seeking Bourbon and branch and I beckoned him and introduced Fred.

"This is the recently missing Representative Fred Olean," I said.

The senator nodded and the two men shook hands, measuring each other. Each seemed pleased with what he surveyed.

"Don here thought you might have fallen asleep in some public bar when you were reported missing," the senator said and sighed. "He said that if that was true you'd never be found until the supply ran out."

Fred shook his head. "I was a man of sober habits until I

came into this session and met Donald Robak." He watched us with sorrowful eyes. "Now, if I'm not out leading a protest march he has me in his rooms making gasoline cocktails that he sells during the nights to the college students."

I ignored both of them. "Did you find out anything of interest about Link, Senator?" I asked.

He shook his head. "Not really. You can hear a hundred stories, but no one has the red-eyed word. If Link introduced anti-pollution so that he could thereafter kill it for a price, there isn't any outstanding, foolproof indication of it. He appeared to be all for it. A lot of them think the price wasn't right yet." He looked away and surveyed the room and back again. "I talked to some pretty astute old heads over in the senate. No one would admit to knowing anything for certain. After all of the talking and all of the stories, if I had to guess about it I'd guess that Link was sixty–forty probably in earnest about the bill, Don."

"Thanks, Senator," I said, buoyed. That gave T. J. Toy a good reason. "Anything else of interest?"

He shook his head. "Not yet."

I stood there and thought and something came to me, an avenue I'd not approached, something I should have done.

I said slowly: "Did either of you ever hear about a guy who writes anti-Semitic crank letters to members of the legislature. This guy stamps them all: USE THE NAME OF CHRIST WHEN YOU PRAY, or somesuch."

Fred nodded first. "I've had a few notes from him. He may be anti-Semitic to you, but he doesn't much like black people either. So far he hasn't had anything to say to me to the good."

The senator said softly, "That's old Katie Sands. I thought she was dead. She must be old enough to be dead."

"It's a woman?" I asked incredulously.

125

He nodded.

"And you know her for sure?"

"If it's the same one, and I'll bet it is, then it's Katie Sands. She's been writing crank letters to legislators for thirty years. She's a little crippled woman who runs a sidewalk newsstand right around the corner from the Blue Hotel. At least she used to run it. She's got the big hate for everything we do." He smiled. "Someone got alarmed about her letters years back when I was here. We had the P. O. inspectors check into it and they gave us Katie Sands. She's harmless according to them, or she was harmless then. Just a nut."

"Does she misspell things?" I asked. "Screw up her grammar?"

He nodded. "She doesn't really need to. The inspector who talked to her thought she was bright enough, but a little twisted. She does the misspellings as a part of her crackpot disguise." He smiled. "After the post office people got on her she promised to quit writing letters, but I guess she hasn't. Maybe she can't."

"Captain Carlson needs to know," I said.

The senator nodded. "I'll run him down when I get back to the hotel if you want me to."

"Please do," I asked.

CHAPTER XI

RULE 32. *Only full members of the commit-tees shall have the right of vote on the question of whether a bill held in that committee shall proceed onward to the house floor for further action.*

I took Judy home and kissed her at the door. It was a kind of distracted kiss on her part. She was still living the governor's mansion, still impressed by people she'd met that night. I'd met all of the same people and I was far more impressed with Judy than I was with them.

"Why don't we get married?" I asked again.

She smiled. "And you with a date with another female tomorrow?"

"That's business," I said.

"It may be business to you, but I think it's more than that to her."

"You're really not answering my question, Miss Judy," I said, wanting her.

"I don't know the answer yet." She looked away from me and was silent for a long moment. When she looked back again she was in another world.

"I'll bet I had the nicest fur there tonight," she said, remembering the party again, forgetting me.

I sighed. "You really did," I said tolerantly.

She kissed me for that and I let her go on in to dream of the governor's mansion which, according to the governor, has cold floors, poor ventilation, mice in the pantry, and the wandering, lonely ghost of the last governor who'd retained his honesty, now some hundred years dead.

I got a cab and went to Big Bad Al's. It was the topless joint that was the last place Link and T.J. had visited before heading for the Blue Hotel on Link's last night. I'd meant to go there with Fred Olean after we'd left George's Rendezvous a few nights back, but the hour had gotten late and we hadn't made it.

I took a seat at the bar and ordered Bourbon and water from a dyspeptic-appearing bartender who poured the drink, with competent, frugal hands, watching me carefully all of the time.

The place was only a little more than half-full, which might be the normal crowd. But T.J. had said the place was crowded and *that* had been a week night.

"Ain't I seen you before?" the bartender asked.

"Maybe," I lied. "I was in here once or twice with Sloan Link. You know him."

The name rang a bell with him, but he shook his head and retreated warily away.

I looked after him, trying to catch his eyes, but he refused to look my way so I turned and watched the floor finally. A rather good pianist was playing from a raised bandstand with one of those amplifier pick-ups magnifying the sound of the music. He had a man on drums on one side and a bass player on the other. Three topless waitresses wandered the room keeping drinks industriously filled. They were all attractive girls. I beckoned meaningfully to the nearest one.

She came over and said disdainfully: "The bartender will serve you, sir." She started to bob away.

I stood up and moved closer to her. "Did you know Sloan Link?" I asked to her back.

She hesitated and then turned. "I knew who he was. Carol over there knew him better." She pointed at one of the other two waitresses, a slim, dark girl with rather astonishing pectoral development.

"Would you ask her if she'd talk to me for a moment, please?"

She hesitated again, eyes curious, but then she nodded at me and went on. I saw her whisper to the dark girl and felt their appraising glances as they discussed me. I think they decided I was probably harmless in a crowd. The dark girl came over.

I said: "The other girl said you knew Sloan Link, Carol. I wonder if you remember him being in here last week with T. J. Toy."

She eyed me suspiciously and waited for more information.

"I'm Don Robak," I said. "I was over in the House of Representatives with Sloan. He was a friend and I'm trying to find out what happened to him that night."

She nodded. "I read the papers. Nothing happened to him while he was here. He and I were supposed to go out together after I got off. Let's see, tomorrow would make a week. Seems longer. I read that story and I've been like mashed about it since." She nodded again. Her voice was a little girl's voice. The rest of her had grown up, but not the voice. "We were jammed that night. There'd been a basketball game out at the arena and we had a big crowd after. Sloan and that T.J. were kind of drunkish. They set over against the

129

wall with a couple of guys and their girls—and later Billie Deseret, that's a travel agent. He came in and I set him with them." Her voice slowed. "We never did get to go out that night. Sloan went home with T.J."

"Had you been out with Sloan before that night?" I asked.

She nodded. "Once," she said matter-of-factly. "T.J. fixed us."

I figured she was all of twenty-five, but her age was no longer germane.

"Did T.J. or Sloan know this Billie?"

"No," she said. "I knew him. I sat him with them on purpose. Sloan had been talking about Florida, so when Billie came in I brought him over to their table thinking he could tell Sloan where to go and maybe arrange it. Billie's a travel agent and business hasn't been too good when I asked him, so he could make a buck with Sloan and like help him at the same time."

"I see." I reached in my billfold and gave her a five dollar bill. She made it disappear and I was afraid to speculate on where she'd disposed of it.

"He does me a favor now and then," she said.

"Did he leave with T.J. and Link?"

She shook her head and the rest solemnly. "No. Billie stayed here. When Sloan went on like that—all drunk—then I went on out with Billie when we got closed here."

Outside the hotel I walked down the street and around the corner. There was one of those flimsy newsstand houses there and a little sign on the top of it read KATIE SANDS. It was long closed for the night. The wind outside was cold and the moon had gone behind heavy clouds.

I wasn't sleepy so I got out the list of bills missing from Link's room that Captain Carlson had furnished me. I sat in my hotel room with the wind howling up a storm outside and carefully went over the list checking it against a master list published (with snide editorial comment) by the Capitol City *Enquirer*. It took about an hour and my eyes were finally getting heavy when I got done.

There were about fifty bills missing from the pile in Link's room, for what significance that incident had. Among the missing was anti-pollution, cross-state power, student-tuition increase and such other highly suspicious items as the budget bill, a measure that would have validated all bonds issued in the past year, a measure to change the middle initial in the name given a state park and suchlike. When I was done with the cross-checking I was as puzzled as when I began.

Outside my hotel window I could now see heavy snow falling and I sat and stared out at the falling snow and thought about Link. It seemed to me that Captain Carlson must be right. It had to be T. J. Toy. Maybe he'd managed to get someone in Link's room as I believed he'd managed to get someone in Olean's. And T.J. had taken Link out that night. Maybe a lot of money was involved, an offer T.J. had made. So Link had gone for a new bottle to celebrate. Then T.J. had killed him with the idea of economizing. Maybe this . . .

Maybe that.

I slept and dreamed. In the dream Link was trying to get in the pearly gates. When they wouldn't let him in he . . .

Somehow Judy got in the dream too and it became a good dream.

I was sorry when morning came.

The snow outside was deep on the ground. The doorman nodded wisely and said: "Fourteen inches." The newsstand was closed.

I went back to the room and got my arctics and my heavi-

131

est coat and mushed out for breakfast. I ate with Fred Olean.

The first thing he asked was: "Where's my two thousand dollars?"

I shrugged.

"A thousand?" he said, prepared to settle.

I shook my head.

"A hundred?"

"What's your rock-bottom price, cash money," I asked.

"Figuring your total net worth," he said, "how about three dollars American?" He watched me sharply. "Anything happen on it yet?"

"No," I said. "I keep hoping something will, but when night comes and I'm in that hotel room I've got all the locks on the door."

"Be careful," he said.

I nodded. "I'll try."

We walked to the Statehouse together. Slogged might be a better word. Traffic crept through the streets and cabdrivers cursed each other.

In the legislative halls a lobbyist I knew and admired beckoned me.

I put my ear down close to his mouth and listened. Everyone does it that way for some reason. Maybe lobbyists think someone else is eavesdropping at their very shoulders, but I've seen them, when there isn't a soul within shouting distance and they want to impart a message to you, have you bend an ear to it.

He said: "The word's out all around that T. J. Toy is the one who engineered the Fred Olean thing."

"Who told you that?" I asked.

He shrugged. "I've been here half an hour and already eight people have told me." He ticked off a bunch of names without hesitation. "So I guess it's all over," he finished.

"Thanks," I said. "Thanks a lot."

I went to the typing room and got a typist to make me enough copies of a notice to members of the Judiciary so that one could be delivered to each member. The notice read: "The Judiciary Committee will have a closed, important meeting in Room C36 on adjournment this date to consider the following bills: H.B. 1732; H.B. 2178; H.B. 2426. We will consider other legislation as time permits."

The three particularly noted were anti-pollution, cross-state power, and the tuition rise.

I delivered the notice to the head page and asked for receipts from all of the legislative addressees. That would stop my friend with the eraser who'd wiped out my last meeting. Sending the notices was the way Sloan had told me to do it. He'd even given me some cuter tricks which I wasn't going to use. You could wait until late afternoon and have your notes delivered in the dusk, leaving out any committee member or members you didn't want present by not sending them the notes.

There were nine members of my Judiciary Committee. In addition, by virtue of their offices, Speaker McGuire, Chapell as minority leader and Polsen as majority leader were ex officio members of all committees and I suspected I might see from one to all of them at the afternoon meeting. I sent them notes.

Someone, maybe it was Link, once told me that a committee could actually be controlled by three members. He used the following reasoning: Five of the nine members of a committee made a quorum and few committees operated with more than a bare quorum as all legislators served on several committees. I, for example, served on Banks Committee and also on Courts Committee. So if you made a quorum of five then three could control the vote. That meant that if in the afternoon I wound up with but five there then I could get Fred Olean, who was a member, to make the necessary motions, trade for a second, then with my own vote to break ties I could win every vote.

I sent a page down with a note for Fred.

The house had opened and an angry argument on a fluoridation measure was occurring. A bill had been introduced to fluoridate the state waters at all state parks and the enemies of fluoridation were now in hot pursuit. I'd gotten letters from my local dentists favoring the measure and a nasty letter from a local chiropractor against it. I still wasn't sure about it, so I tried to listen.

I could see Fred. His chair was turned diagonally. He received the note from the page. He looked at me and winked. In a little bit, while the fight was moving good on the floor with conflicting statistics being quoted, he slipped out of his seat and into Link's vacant seat.

"What do you have in the Judiciary that you want out?" I asked.

He thought for a minute. "I haven't really got a thing, but the senator from my district has been agonizing with me on a change of venue bill that would allow his county to venue into additional counties other than the three small counties that surround our large one." He nodded. "I could be a real hero with him and make some points if I could tell him I'd unbottled that little bill. I imagine I might even use getting it out for trading. He's got some stuff of mine he's sitting on over there that's already passed this house."

"Trade him," I said. "Tell him his venue bill is as good as out of committee labeled 'do pass' as of this afternoon."

"Okay," he said. "I'm waiting. I've had the long, slow curve. When do I find out about the fast ball?"

I grinned. "Now," I said, "here's what I want you to do. . . ."

He listened and nodded and grinned back.

After he was gone I called upon two more members of my committee while the water was still being fluoridated.

I did some trading.

Both agreed to go along with the motions of Fred Olean without deviation or question.

I agreed to unbury for the first legislator a packaging measure desired by someone in his jurisdiction. The other wanted me to bury deep a measure which called for a constitutional amendment barring the use of federal taxes for other uses than in this country. It was a bill that was, I understand, perennially introduced, perennially buried. But it was a crazy year and legislator number two was worried about it. It was a cheap trade.

At a little after five that afternoon I opened my first meeting of the Judiciary Committee as chairman. Outside the snow was still blowing. The meeting room seemed warm, but the wind outside was cold enough to make the areas near the windows frigid. We sat around a long conference table. An attractive girl from the stenographic pool took notes.

I was glad I'd dealt for a fourth vote because we had seven members present and none of them acted as if they were about to leave. In addition to the seven we had Polsen and Chapell. Speaker McGuire had hovered around the door for a few moments talking to Polsen, but had gone on and not reappeared.

T. J. Toy was sitting over on the side of the room. All of the other lobbyists had left.

I rapped on the table with knuckles and turned to look at T.J.

"As announced in the notices, Mr. Toy, this is a closed meeting."

"I don't see why that should apply to me," he said. "I'd like to be here when House Bill 1732 is voted on. That's first on your agenda." He shook his head nervously.

"Again," I said, "I'll tell you this is a closed meeting and ask you to leave."

"Can I talk to you for a moment in the corridor?" he said, rising.

I thought about it. "After the meeting. Right now your best bet would be to send me a telegram."

I heard a couple of snickers down the conference table. T.J. rose and went to the door. I locked it behind him ignoring his hostile glances. I'd been mean and spiteful and I was feeling pretty good about it right at that moment.

I sat back down and said: "First bill that we're to consider is House Bill 1732, the anti-pollution measure. I note from the records which were kindly acquired for us by Representative Polsen"—I nodded to him and got a smile—"that there has been adequate discussion on the measure before. If there's no cogent new argument then I'll entertain a motion."

Several hands went up. I recognized Fred's.

"I move the bill be released from this committee recommended 'do pass' and that the name of Donald Robak be substituted for the name of the previous author, Sloan Link."

"Thank you," I said. "I'll accept the burden of authorship." I continued to ignore the flapping hands. "All in favor?"

"Let's have some discussion," Chapell said, his voice sarcastic.

"Representative Chapell," I said, "I've ended discussion of the bill in the committee." I looked around. "Once again —all in favor?"

Fred's hand went up and so did my faithful two. Three votes for.

"And opposed?" I asked.

Five hands went up including Chapell's and Polsen's.

"Three against," I said. "I vote for release and the motion. The bill shall be released with a recommendation for passage."

"I counted five votes against the bill," Chapell said testily.

I smiled gently. "You're a member ex officio, Representative Chapell. So is Representative Polsen. You have no votes here. I counted the voting members. I'd suggest you read rule 32."

I thought he was going to become angry, but he controlled himself with some difficulty. Polsen smiled at me.

"He sat long enough next to Link that the rules have rubbed off on him," he said to Chapell.

Chapell gave me an ominous look. "We'll get to the bill when it comes up for vote."

"I'd suggest you read the rules on when and if it can now come up for vote," I said. "That's if you're not familiar with them already."

Then, in rapid succession, with my name substituted for Link's as author we released for passage the cross-state power bill and the student-tuition hike. Polsen asked to have his name shown as author of the cross-state power bill instead of mine. His request was low voiced, reasonable.

"No," I said, when he was done. "I suspect I'd better be the author listed on the bill. You know the rules for calling down bills, Representative Polsen. I'm trying to substitute myself for Link wherever possible. I think I can carry Link's bills. And with the rules being that only the listed author can call down a bill for final vote, then I'm going to insist on having the say-so on these bills."

Polsen smiled back, but Chapell's eyes were yellow.

They left before we voted on any of the bills I was paying my debts with. Outside in the hall I saw Chapell pause and fall into conversation with T. J. Toy.

CHAPTER XII

RULE 37. *In the house of its introduction only the author of a bill, or his substitute, may call that bill down for its reading upon passage.*

I picked up Gertrude May at her office. She was wearing high boots against the snow. I helped her into a fur coat which Judy would have been smug about because it wasn't as nice or as rich as Judy's. I reflected that if Judy did become Mrs. Donald Robak her coat would get old before it would get anything else—like replaced.

We walked down marble stairs that had seen so much pedestrian traffic that they were worn into grooves. In the foyer of the Statehouse our steps echoed against the emptiness of the building. My committee had been the last to finish.

"If you want to see a lonely place at night," Gertrude said, "then you wait until they start having night sessions in a week or so. Be the last one out. Just hope against hope the Statehouse Shehogies don't get you."

On the steps we passed T. J. Toy. He ignored me and plunged on into the building. I was a lost cause to him now.

"I wonder where he's going?" I said.

"To call down the Shehogies on your head," she said flippantly. "Where are we going?"

"I'll let you choose."

I followed her by taking her arm and letting her lead. The snow was falling lightly. The streets had been cleared, but the sidewalks were still packed high. A smog of industrial smoke lay over the city making it hard to breathe, quickly overlaying the fallen snow with a sheen of brown.

She led me to an old bar. The front of the place was made of old-fashioned windows and faded wood. A non-neon sign on the front read: NERO'S.

Inside there were warm steam tables and the fragrance exuding from them was tantalizing. She went haughtily past them and I followed. To the rear and through a passageway there was a barroom filled with sturdy wood tables and chairs. It was about half-full and we found a secluded table. An attentive waiter in a somber black suit and antiseptic linen took our drink order.

"This place has been here a hundred years," she said. "My first husband and I had dinner here on our honeymoon." She sighed and nodded her head. "The food is good and prices are reasonable. I'm trying to save you money, Don." She smiled a little smile. "And wait'll you see the size of the drinks."

She was right. The waiter brought us drinks that were really something. Hers was scotch and water and mine was Bourbon and the same. Mine was in a big glass tumbler and it was dark and strong with good Bourbon.

"Great," I said appreciatively.

"Sloan was fond of it." She sighed. "Fire away. I saw the competition last night. It made me figure there was probably only one reason why you were taking me out and that was to quiz me. So I'm trading the quiz session for some good drinks and maybe a meal."

"Whatever you want," I said. "But it isn't that way," I said gently and not completely truthfully.

She brightened a bit. "Go ahead anyway," she said.

"Tell me more about Link," I said. "I find I knew him without knowing him. Maybe you've got some ideas about what happened. Maybe you know about how he lived, how he got the money to pay the bills. Something you know might help me figure out why he was killed and who killed him."

She sipped at her drink. Her voice, when it finally came, was hesitant: "I don't really know much that you don't know. He never said anything about money, but there always seemed to be plenty." She grimaced. "I've heard the stories about him. Maybe they were true, maybe not. He lived by his own rules. When I was going with him he wanted to retire. Someplace by the sea. He'd never really been anywhere, Don. Between sessions he lived in his little town up there and he came down here for sessions, but this was the top of the world for him—at least until this session." She smiled, remembering. "Always before, there were things I could do. I showed him places here he'd never seen—like Nero's. I even started him at trying to dress half decent. He could have been a handsome man." She shook her head. "Maybe not handsome—distinguished. I was willing to forget what had happened, go on as we'd been before. When this session began I thought it would be that way. Then he began to shy away, pick at me, start a fight whenever I came around. He was a good schemer. Sometimes I thought he looked harried when I'd see him. I think it was mostly that he was going hard to get something this time—as if this was going to be his last time here and he wasn't going to waste

141

any of it." Her voice lowered. "I guess he really had something going this time."

"Anti-pollution?" I queried.

"Maybe. I hear there's lots of money around on that." She watched me carefully. "I think he had plans for you, Don Robak. He was very good at using people and I think he was going to use you. He always picked a bright new one."

"For what?" I asked.

She shrugged. "Who knows. Sloan wasn't the most direct man the world ever saw. I've seen him running five or six bills so that he could trade them all and get one thing done that no one suspected him of being interested in. He was very, very sharp."

Sharp enough to cut his own throat, I thought.

I said: "I liked him. He had time enough to spare for me. Time's a rare gift these days. Not many have it and those who do usually don't want to let it go."

She smiled. "I think eventually he might have had you doing most of the work, Don. When you were with him remember that you only saw the surface of his iceberg, the part he wanted you to see. He'd never have let you know what was under the water."

I shrugged, without fully believing or disbelieving what she said. I remembered Link's often-repeated statement that you could do almost anything in the legislature if you knew the rules. I knew those rules and they operated the same for everyone. I thought they'd been the same for Link.

I asked: "Did he tell you anything that night in the Blue Hotel bar? Anything at all?"

She hesitated for a long moment. "I said before that he didn't and I suppose I ought to leave it that way. He was drunk. He called me a name and he gave me that old grin. Then he said: 'Bitch, I've got half a million reasons why

I can't and won't talk to you.' Then he just pushed on past and I let him go."

"Bitch?" I asked. "Is that the name he called you?"

She nodded. "It's part of an old joke that never was very good." She shook her head. "It was a private thing and means nothing here."

"Please?" I asked.

But she shook her head and was so resolute that I was afraid of losing her.

I asked: "What did he mean by the half a million reasons?"

"Maybe money," she said. "Maybe nothing at all. He expressed himself much of the time in numbers. It was a hundred of this and a thousand of that and a million here and a billion there." She shook her head. "I doubt that it was money, really. If he'd had that kind of money treed, I'd have known about it."

I shook my head and she watched the gesture curiously.

"How much money is Chapell's wife worth?" I asked.

"No," she said, with finality.

"How much?" I insisted.

"I've heard everything from half a million up to a top of a couple of million."

"That's a lot of money," I said.

She smiled and shook her head. "I don't think Sloan could take her even with a couple of million. He told me they'd once had an affair years back. I guess he broke it off when she started taking charge. He told me that she wanted to immediately run him for governor or U. S. Senator. Then she wanted to stop him drinking. That last must really have shook him up. The affair didn't last long and it was many years back. I don't think Sloan fooled with her after that. In the past few years he's had a thing about youth. He became about like the television ads. The only time they ever want anyone over thirty is when they're trying to sell pills or suppositories."

I smiled and nodded. Gertrude chattered on. Her talk lost my immediate interest.

Sometimes I'd thought Link a lonely man. His life was sterile and without variance. He knew his job and he talked and lived his job all of the time. He had warmth and presence, but he had little other conversation except for his store of off-color jokes. In reality the legislature and Maker's Mark made up his life.

There were other legislators who were the same way. Polsen was similar. His life was sterile. Chapell's seemed to fall in the same groove except for his rich wife.

It was hard for me to believe Link willingly leaving the legislature.

After a while, when Gertrude's rapid-fire conversation slowed, we ordered steaks. They were so good that I over-tipped. That was something Link had told me never to let happen unless a lobbyist was paying.

I went back to the Blue Hotel and on to my room and I waited there. I stayed up, sitting in my one good chair, dozing now and then.

It was still early in the night. Outside my window I could see the blossoming lights of the dirty, busy city.

I got the phone directory out from the night stand and looked through it. There was a number for the Deseret Travel Agency and another for a Deseret, W. I tried the office number first and got no answer so I dialed the other number.

"Billie Deseret," the voice at the other end answered. It was a pleasant voice eager for whatever I had in mind. A voice for our times.

"This is Representative Donald Robak," I said. "I'm trying to run down whatever I can about Representative Sloan Link. I understand you met him the night he was killed?"

"That's right," he said, cooling, "but I'm afraid I can't help you much. I'd never met the man before that night. A girl I know sat me with him at a bar and I talked to him for a bit. He wasn't making much sense. He was pretty drunk and so was the fat guy with him. Really bombed."

"Were they arguing?" I asked.

"No, sir," he said emphatically. "The fat guy was buying the table drinks and this other big guy was lapping them up as fast as Carol, she's the waitress I know, could bring them. But everything was friendly. I talked to Representative Link about Florida before he got too far along and sold him on the west coast. I think it's a better deal. The east coast is too built up now. He wanted a place to go. I got him two weeks to look the scene over by making a call right while he was there. Nice motel place on the ocean near Naples. He followed me out to the pay phone when I called." He stopped for a moment. "He'd have loved the place."

"Did he pay you for it?"

"That isn't the way it usually works," he said, a little stiffly. "I'd have gotten a percentage back from the place I sold him on—they'd have paid me. He did give a deposit though. I suppose I'll have to give it back now if they ask." His voice became hesitant. "That poor man had never even been to Florida. He'd sure have liked it down there this time of year. All he could talk about was how cold it was up here."

"How much of a deposit?" I asked.

"A hundred dollars," he said. "He acted a little funny about it. He didn't want the fat guy to know about it when we made the call or when he gave me the money. He gave me the hundred back in the john. I mailed him a receipt. He told me to mail it to his home address." His voice took on a note of chagrin. "I'd mailed it to him before I found out he was dead."

"Did he say why he didn't want the fat guy to see him give you the money?"

"No, sir," he said.

"Is there anything else you remember about it?"

"No, sir," he said again firmly.

I thanked him and hung the phone up. I sat there and tried to figure out why Link wouldn't have wanted T.J. to see him give money to Billie Deseret, the friendly travel agent. The most obvious reason was that T.J. had given money to Sloan and perhaps warned him about openly spending it because of the harmful talk it might cause. But I couldn't see T.J. doing that. T.J. had as much brass as a marching band and a hundred wasn't that much money. A second answer could be that someone else had given the money to Link and he didn't want T.J. to know there were other bidders. A third could be that he just didn't want T.J. to know his business because T.J. had a big mouth.

Thinking about that, I fell into a doze and didn't come back awake for a time. Outside it had grown still with only an occasional siren slicing the night.

I listened for the phone. It seemed to me that someone must call me. I'd taken over Link's bills and I'd taken over his position of legislative authority. I controlled all that he'd controlled. Without me none of the three warm bills could become law. I had to call those bills down for a vote. Trouble was that I didn't know whether that shadowy someone wanted those bills called down or wanted them killed. I was leading Link's life without Link's knowledge.

Someplace that night I presumed that student activists were ramming pins into effigies of me or maybe using my campaign posters for dart boards. I was supposed to be their lad and I'd taken their bill out of committee for a vote on the floor. I wondered if anyone around the student headquarters had bothered to try to figure my reasons and thought they'd probably not done any figuring. I also doubted that anyone knew I personally had to call the bill down for a vote. The rule was, if not obscure, at least unfamiliar to laymen.

I wondered at myself and tried to analyze my reasons. It wasn't bravery. I've given up hope on that. I think I was doing it in a sort of anger. Someone had thought it wise to kill Link, probably hoping to profit from the act of killing. I was angry because I was Link and Link was me. Link's death made my world insecure and to renew it I had to dig on. Besides, I'd always owned a gnawing curiosity. And I was curious about what was happening, about the smell of corruption. I knew my own state. The fact that corruption existed wasn't something that surprised me.

I went to sleep finally. In the dream I was on one of those brilliant white beaches they have in Florida—a beach as yet untouched by oil slicks, maybe the last pristine beach. I was sitting there with a big drink in my hand and the sun was hot above me. Link was laughing at me and in the dream I knew why he was laughing. He had a little hand bell and he kept laughing and ringing it at me.

I came awake and only the bell was true. The telephone was ringing. I felt myself break into a cold sweat and I reached gingerly for the phone.

"Robak," I said to the phone receiver.

"This is Captain Carlson," the voice said and I recognized it and relaxed. "I know it's late, but we caught one of the people who kidnaped your buddy, Olean. We've been working it pretty good and we found your Mr. Toy a few steps back. Seems he hired the guy who hired the one we have in custody. There's a pick-up order out on Toy now. We lost him earlier tonight, but we've got a man watching the place where he's staying. And we've got statements from the two people who can tie Toy into the thing." He stopped for a moment. "I thought you'd want to know. It's only a matter of time until we catch him."

"Thanks," I said. "Thanks a lot." I was now almost fully awake.

"If it means anything," Carlson said slowly, "the guy we first picked up said in his statement that they were going to mail a letter after the anti-pollution bill was passed telling where Representative Olean was. He said they weren't supposed to hurt him. Of course, that's easy now, but I will say that no one who's involved, other than Toy, has a past record for violent crimes."

"How about Toy's record?" I asked.

"He was convicted of voluntary manslaughter. I talked to a man in the town where the crime was committed. Toy had some kind of fight with a guy in a bar. The other guy was bigger and stronger. He beat Toy up pretty badly and Toy drew a gun and shot him, killed him. He did about two years and made parole. Technically he was in violation of the parole, but they weren't really looking for him and aren't interested in extraditing him."

"I see." Something else came to me. "Did you check out the newsstand lady who writes the nasty letters?"

"Yes," he said. "She wears a full-time wheel chair and she's about eighty years old, Don. She can't be involved. I think she phrased the letter that way accidentally or because she's a vicious old broad and hoped someone had pushed Representative Link out his window."

"Okay," I said. "I'll take your word for it. One more thing while I've got you. What did you find out around the Blue Hotel that I don't know about?"

"Not much," he said. "I checked out the maid that tried the door and there wasn't anything doing that was of any help. I went to see the bartender who gave Link the booze and began talking bent law this and violation that and he got very co-operative. He remembered Link coming down and he remembered that Link was drunk, but the bottle was supposed to go to the room, so he sold him. He said Link fumbled around for a while, then got a twenty out of his billfold. He gave it to the bartender and didn't wait for change. Then he talked for just a minute to a woman the bartender identified as Gertrude May. He knows her because he'd seen her in there before with Link. Link left and the woman stayed. According to the bartender she was still there when the place closed, which was after Link went out the window. He says she might have left and come back, but he didn't think so."

"Okay," I said. I thought for a minute. "If you want to find Toy you might have them try the bars out along the strip. If they've got a girl inside with most of her clothes off then that's T.J.'s kind of place."

"It's after three in the morning," he said righteously. "Those places are supposed to be closed." He paused. "We might try some of the after-hours places though."

"If any of them have strippers as a part of the menu, start there," I said.

After I rehung the phone I lay down on the bed, but the pursuit of sleep was difficult.

T. J. Toy had tried to use reverse psychology to defeat anti-pollution. He'd figured the legislature would quickly rescind the passage of the bill and bury it deep. He'd been ruthless enough to take advantage of the chaos the students had brought with them in their marches.

I wondered if he'd been ruthless enough to kill Sloan Link?

Maybe he'd given Link the money to buy the whiskey? He admitted drinking with him, he'd been the last man to see him—known—and I'd never been able to verify the fact that he'd left Link and gone on back to the Athletic Club. And if T.J. could connive and kidnap and buy votes and kill before, then couldn't he kill now?

But Link had gotten the money out of his own billfold according to the bartender. . . .

After a while I wandered off into sleep and back to that white-on-white beach in Florida. There Link laughed at me again, amused over a secret I didn't seem to be able to share.

CHAPTER XIII

RULE 42. *The doorkeepers shall keep order in the halls and upon the premises of the State-house. No loud or boisterous conduct shall be allowed. Any senator or representative assisting loud or boisterous persons shall be subject to disciplinary action by the members of his house.*

In the morning I was badly treated almost first off. All I had time for before was my usual breakfast with Fred Olean. Thereafter we walked on up to the Statehouse.

My student constituents and some from other schools were out in force. All of their signs were held stiffly high and they paraded antagonistically up and down the sidewalk.

But as I drew near in the crisp cold of the morning all sound and motion stopped.

I heard some voices whisper: "There he is." And other voices echoed them risingly, but still no one moved. I was reduced by a repeating of whispered profanities and invitations to illegal acts. I moved on through the line and to the steps. Fred stayed with me.

I saw Harlan Hill. Some of the kids around him were also

recognizable. I'd seen them at the student headquarters or remembered them from the campaign.

I saw Harlan make a small signal with his hand.

Collectively all of them turned their backs on me and stood that way while I went up the Statehouse steps. There must have been a thousand of them.

At the top of the steps a vigilant newsman, probably alerted by Harlan or one of his aides, snapped pictures. I smiled amiably at the camera, but something inside me had already turned to ashes. I guess I thought I deserved the benefit of the doubt. No one gets it these days.

Fred quick-opened the door and sort of powered me through it.

"Whew," he said, wiping his forehead. He looked me over with some disgust. "That was chancy. Why don't you pass the word that no one can call that bill down but you?"

"I'll wait a bit," I said.

"Why? After what you told me at breakfast about the police looking for T. J. Toy I can't see why you'd wait."

The photographer from the top of the steps had followed us inside. He stood watching dubiously and I guess he overheard Fred's remark.

"That could take some waiting," he said loudly.

I turned on him. "Private conversation," I said. "Move it on."

He shrugged amiably and touched his camera. "I've a good picture of you here, Representative Robak. I've got a better one I just took of T. J. Toy. He made an easier subject than you did. I guess you could call him a 'still life.'"

I watched him, uncomprehending.

"He's dead," the photographer said. "They found him in the basement here at the bottom of the stairwell early this morning. You know the one I mean? The big circular stairs that lead up to the legislative chambers and down to a blind wall. He'd either jumped or been pushed over the railing. No one is saying which." He gave me a plaintive look. "Have you got anything to say about it?" He reached into his back pocket and flashed a press card. I liked him better. It wasn't from the *Enquirer*.

Olean moved in front of me. My mouth was open.

"Not yet," Olean said warningly to me.

I shook my head. "Nothing. Better check with the police, Mac."

Olean took my arm again and moved me on leaving the frustrated photographer behind.

We went quickly on to the mentioned steps. A curious crowd moved slowly up them, all looking downward over the edge of the steps. In the basement men still worked taking pictures, measuring and chalking, but I didn't see a body. I did see Captain Carlson standing at the edge of a group who appeared to be supervising the work. His eyes came up as I watched him and met mine. He nodded almost imperceptibly.

"I'll be up in a few minutes," I said to Fred. I walked on down the steps. At the last landing two state officers guarded the last flight of steps, but they parted for me at a nod from Carlson. He stood waiting for me.

"I just got here a little bit ago," he said apologetically. "I tried to call your hotel, but you'd already gone."

I nodded and stood next to him and looked the scene below over. There was a chalked area on the floor. Somehow it seemed smaller than T.J. had ever been. I thought I saw darker stains on the old, dark floor.

Carlson reached in his pocket and handed me a note.

"This is a copy of the note that we found in his coat

pocket," he said. "The real one's gone on to the laboratory to be checked, but I made a copy." He handed it to me.

It was typed and it read: "They're after me. I heard it on the police band. I shouldn't have done it. Now this is the only way out."

It was unsigned.

I said: "Anyone could have typed that."

He nodded. "It was on the police radio and even on some local-news stations late that we were looking for him. He could have heard it. I agree that anyone could have typed the note, though."

"Any chance of identifying the typewriter it was typed on?"

"I figure there's maybe a thousand here in the Statehouse, but we'll check." He nodded to himself, trying for belief. "If he'd done any investigating himself he'd have pretty easily found out that we had two of his people in jail and statements on the kidnaping of your friend, Olean."

"When did he die?"

"Before I called you this morning. We put out a dispatch to pick him up about eleven last night. The coroner's assistant thought he died sometime after midnight and before two this morning. He was wearing a watch. If it had stopped we might have had an exact time, but it was still running."

He looked around. "There isn't anything down here at the bottom of the stairwell. These steps used to lead to the old legislative caucus rooms, but when the remodeling and rebuilding was done ten years back, they added the old rooms to the administrative offices and closed off the entrances down here so that the steps just led down to nothing." He looked at the blank walls around him. "See how it narrows?" he asked. "He was hid pretty well under the overhang. I imagine it would have had to have been full day before he was found, but a janitor left a bucket down here. He came down to get it two hours ago and found Toy."

"Are you going to call it a suicide?" I asked.

His face was complacent, but there was a toughness in his eyes that I'd never share or know. "It would solve a lot of problems for all of us. It's an apparent answer, a solution. Toy knew his record would come out and he'd be ruined. So he takes a swan dive over the rail. It was the way he killed Link. Maybe he thought there was some kind of justice in going the same way."

I watched him and understood partly. He wasn't really satisfied, but he was trying it on again and hoping for a fit.

I remembered what he'd told me about Link. "Did he have any unexplained injuries?" I asked, pointing to the chalked spot.

He shook his head. "He had massive head injuries, but they weren't unexplained. He hit headfirst. I imagine they'll plant him with the casket closed." He inspected me without affection or rancor. "Let's say that this one's up in the air, Don. We haven't given any statement to the newspapers yet on any theory. All I know now is that Toy is dead." He rubbed hard at the scar on his face as if remembering an old mistake. "I don't take much for granted any more."

I nodded, satisfied.

I left him and walked on up the steps to the legislative floor. Curious eyes inspected me and I felt them. At the top of the steps Speaker McGuire fell in beside me and patted me on the back. He was wearing a careful smile.

"I suppose it's wrong to be glad anyone's dead," he said softly, so that no one could overhear. "I'm sorry for T.J., but it does solve some problems here." He nodded amiably at me. "I'll give you your due in the matter, young man. You're the one who got the job done. It was an inspiration to put you in Link's job and on the committee to look into his passing." He patted my back again with a hand as heavy as fate. "You may have done me a turn towards electing me a U. S. Senator."

He turned away and went jovially down the hall. I watched him curiously as he called out to various lobbyists. He stopped to talk to one for a small moment and then proceeded to the hall that led to his office.

Polsen and Chapell, the gold-dust twins, moved close to me. They were watching him also.

Polsen smiled the good smile: "His heaviness seems to be in a most happy mood."

"Yup," I said without inflection. "A funny thing happened this date. A man got killed. Very laughable."

Chapell moved in front of me antagonistically. His voice was waspish. "If anyone caused all of the trouble around here it's certainly you. My wife complained to me that you even had the effrontery to ask her some questions. Anyone with that much guts shouldn't be in the legislature." He wasn't very far from sneering. "Why don't you run for sheriff down in that podunk county of yours?"

I smiled. "Might be a good way of getting straight. Better and with more hope of redemption than being a legislator."

Chapell reddened. Polsen put his head back and brayed. I walked away and left them.

All of that day I sat in a fog. Around me the legislature pursued its time-worn ways. Speaker McGuire and the authors of bills had scheduled a number of fairly noncontroversial bills. It was the kind of day a lazy man like me should have enjoyed. I didn't enjoy it. I spent the time sitting there in my broad chair in a daze, living the session over, digging holes in my own memory about what had happened.

On the floor legislators made the pitch for their bills. I heard the old phrase over and over: "It's a good bill," the pleader would importune, "and should pass."

Midway in the afternoon we had a bomb scare. A caller to the house switchboard warned that the bomb was due off in ten minutes. He asked that all legislators be warned with the exception of Donald Robak.

I got the story from one of the door guards.

It didn't take long for it to spread around the floor when we reconvened. It was nice to be loved.

There wasn't any bomb.

Maybe there'd be one next time.

After that the longer I sat there the worse I felt. I knew that nothing was finished yet.

I wanted to crowd up close in my wide wing-backed chair so that I'd make a small target. So I sat there and pieced it out again and again, trying to see how it fit, having a hunch that might be the final hunch. I saw some things that I really should have seen before.

I got notes from around the floor asking when I was going to call down all three of my hot bills. The house militants wanted to pull down the bill on the raise of tuition. Maybe they knew what had happened to me that morning and thought it would be a good time. I wrote temporizing answers to the notes and had them delivered by anxious pages. In truth, I could easily stall, for the bills were only just now back from the printers and until they'd been on the desks of the members of the house for a day couldn't be voted on, unless the rules were suspended.

T. J. Toy was dead. I felt no sense of loss, but I knew that everyone wasn't like me. For that shadowy one who'd killed, the time of crisis seemed over. I looked around the chambers and it seemed to me there must be a way to begin the heat again. Around me other legislators crouched in their broad seats, lost to me except when they turned.

I felt as if I were alone.

Finally, the day's session was done. Despite the fact that Banks Committee was meeting I left the Statehouse immediately, went out a back door, so that I could avoid any lingering students. I hurried through the cold evening and down a busy city alley and into the back door of the Blue Hotel. I went on up to the Law-lobby room and got myself a drink. I sat there and nursed it. I made some calls. I called Captain Carlson, who thought I was pretty incredible, but was willing to go along for the ride. I called Harlan Hill, who was cool to the whole idea until some obvious matters were explained. I called my partner, Senator Adams, who was, all things considered, pretty much of a captive audience.

After that I read that day's copy of the Capitol City *Enquirer*. Some generous or discriminating person had left one lying on a table in the lobby room. Around me, as I read, the noisy party came to life again.

The paper noted that an "obscure lobbyist," one T. J. Toy, had been found dead and that police were still speculating on the cause of his death. "Toy was being sought," the paper matter-of-factly reported, "for questioning about the recent abduction of a state legislator, which many key figures still attribute to student terrorists, and also about the earlier, probable suicide death of another." That was all there was. A blob. I was glad I hadn't expected much.

Sometimes I wondered about the people who ran that paper. I wondered if they sat around in some overstuffed editorial room deciding the fate of the state and what of that fate they could report. There wasn't going to be anything reported that could hurt the paper's favorite party and also nothing that could help the other political side. Some days, it seemed to me, that might leave half the sports page and most of the comics.

Judy came. I'd been watching for her. She was dressed in pink, pink sweater, darker pink skirt. An admiring bartender gave her a drink and she came on over to me, ignoring other inviting eyes.

"Did I meet that man who died?" she asked in a low voice.

"We met him that night we went around to all of the strip places," I said. "T. J. Toy."

She shook her head and I thought she lost a little color. She said: "I heard someone had been killed and that he was a lobbyist, but no one knew the name in my office. I wondered if it were possible . . ."

She looked away from me, not really wanting to come to grips with it any more.

I forced her back to it. "He either jumped over the steps or someone threw him over them. My bet is that he was thrown over."

"Why?" she asked. She shook her head. "Why is it that you always believe the worst?"

I smiled a little. "People jump off bridges and buildings and mountains and cliffs. I never heard of anyone jumping down a stairwell."

"Maybe it was an accident," she said.

I shook my head, determined to make her face the fact that all is not always well in life. I said: "I looked at those steps. A guy my size, if he was extremely uncareful and very drunk, might manage to fall over. But T.J. was a lot shorter than me. The railing on those steps would have hit him pretty far above his center of gravity."

She nodded, still not very happy about it. "Are we going to do anything tonight?" she asked.

I smiled down at her. "I called the governor and he wanted us to come out for another party. Then I told him you weren't going to wear your coat and it was all off."

"Come on," she said smiling back at me.

I waited until her eyes fell. "I'm going to get you another drink in a few minutes," I said. "Then, in a little while, I'm going to put you in a cab and send you home. After you're there I'd like it if you'd lock the doors and stay in and keep young Alex in."

This time her face visibly whitened. "It's all over, isn't it, Don? Why do you want me to do that?"

"I hope it will finish tonight," I said lightly. "Some loose ends only. I don't want you to be involved." I held up my hand at her half-formed protest. "No danger for me," I lied. "There'll be people around me—police. I just want to make sure that you keep Alex safe."

She shivered. "I want us all safe, Don." She shook her head. "You're not a policeman, Don. Let the police do whatever needs to be done." She looked around the room where the party had now moved into second gear. "I'm not very brave, Don."

"Neither am I," I said and laughed. "Just stay in tonight. No matter who calls or comes to the door, don't open it. Even if they claim to have a message from me or from your ex-husband, don't open the door." I touched her hand and it was trembling a little and I was sorry to frighten her, but two people had died. "I doubt if anyone would try to use you to bargain, but then they took Fred."

She nodded and retrieved her hand. She drank the rest of her drink quickly. Her lips never really got all their color back. She refused another drink and I took her down and entrusted her to a balding, husky cabdriver. It was still light outside, but I gave the driver extra money to escort her to the door and asked him to wait until he knew she was safe inside.

She left without kissing me good-bye.

I went up to my own room. Inside I made a final telephone call.

I asked for a hundred thousand.

I thought maybe Representative Sloan Link had maybe asked for half a million, which had been too much. Now Link was dead.

My room was refused as a meeting place. I refused some places he named. Finally he came up with the legislative chamber at eleven o'clock. The floor would be deserted. I'd thought he'd eventually name the chamber and so I agreed.

I sat in my big chair and made a few more calls to people I'd already talked to. I was tired and half sick inside. The world had soured for me. I'd had the feeling before, but its loss and cure had built no immunity for its return. I wanted to go back to Bington, where I could color in my law books on rainy days.

CHAPTER XIV

RULE 71. No legislator shall challenge any person to a duel. Any legislator issuing such a challenge shall be expelled from the legislature upon proof to the presiding officer thereof.

The north doors of the Statehouse are ever open. I used them. Because I had worried as I walked through the cold night to the Statehouse I used the north steps instead of the previously deadly spiral steps. It was disconcerting that route also. Only a few lights were on and there were pools of shadows that seemed endless. Places for Gert's Statehouse Shehogies to hide.

I thought my immediate safety, on the way to my meeting, wasn't in much danger. I was sure he'd want to question me, determine what I knew, who I might have confided in, before he took any new steps. The trouble with that assumption was that two men were dead and I wasn't sure.

I went on to the legislative chamber. There was enough light in the corridors to make the journey possible. I'd promised to make no additional light myself so that the single night guard would not be drawn. That poor man had a lot of building to patrol without bothering with me. Once before, when I'd been in the building late, I'd seen him patrolling. That night he'd been vigorously after the job from a couch in a deserted office. Someday they'll blow the Statehouse down and then we'll go to three guards.

I saw no one.

I went on into the chamber and sat in one of the front chairs and waited. It was dark, but there was enough light so that the chamber was outlined. In the back of the chamber I could hear the creak as some of the huge chairs swung loosely in an invisible wind. Somewhere close a window was open and the room was cold. I could hear the night noises of the old Statehouse around me and I could hear the sounds that penetrated that open window as traffic moved in the night outside.

So I sat there and listened, afraid to see whether anyone had taken me seriously and whether my plan had anyone other than myself really involved.

It wasn't very long.

"Hello," he said easily from the door. I was startled. He'd come upon me unaware for all of my listening and watching.

He was wearing a smile, but his eyes were wary. He came on in and stood near me and used that vantage point to look all around. There was nothing to see except the soldier-like rows of seats, nothing to hear but the night noises, but his eyes told me he really didn't like all of this room, all of this open territory.

"I didn't bring any witnesses," I jibed. I smiled back at him. "I decided we'd both be better off without them."

He gave me a tiny sneer. "You've got a most conceited idea of your value, Robak," he said. "I can get done what I want done without you ever letting my bill come down for passage."

"Perhaps," I said idly. "I know the rules also. Maybe you

could take a bill that'd passed the senate and gut it after the enacting clause and try to write your own bill into it. Maybe you could add it on in some committee where you could put the heat on. Maybe you could get appointed to a conference committee, where disputes are settled between house and senate versions of a bill, and write it in there." I shook my head. "The trouble is that I'd be watching you all of the time and it would be chancy. The odds would be against you and you have to have the bill."

He looked away from me, alert at some tiny noise from the hall, but nothing else came, so he looked back. The cords in his neck were bunched and tight. He said: "I could maybe get the people who are interested to get you like five thousand, maybe even as much as ten," he said. "Then they could appoint you as special counsel or something down there in Bington and maybe pay you five or ten more a year for a while." He shook his head. "But a hundred thousand right now is just out of the question."

"Link asked for half a million, didn't he?"

He surveyed me coolly, but the muscles were still tight. He shook his head in negation. I was sure from his eyes that I was right.

"I never talked to Link about it," he said. "Me and Link, we killed a fatted calf a time or two along the way, but this one's mine."

I smiled. "We're going to have to be honest with each other. You need me and I need your money. I wouldn't have figured it out about the money if I hadn't been able to add it up in my mind and make it come out that you killed Link."

"I didn't kill Link," he said softly, eyes shining in the darkness. "We were friends. You know that." He looked warily around the chamber. "I've always thought it was some of your college outlaws that killed him, probably because of

165

that tuition bill he was going to put to them." He shrugged. "Or maybe it was T.J. In any event, it isn't my problem."

"I thought about the college boy idea and discarded it," I said. "I decided that it would have been impossible for a college boy to get into Link's room. He might have let a girl in, but I couldn't see him leaving her, even to get booze. I figured he'd have called the bar and waited. Maybe he wouldn't have waited patiently, but he'd have waited. Link knew the kids hated him. He knew it's a violent world. He had a chance with a girl earlier, two actually, and he wasn't interested." I shook my head. "He wasn't going to let some kid, male or female, in his room, furnish the booze, then drink till fall-over time with a stranger. The kids were just a good stalking horse for the killer. They're getting a lot of bad publicity and so they were useful. I figured the kids as improbables. The odds were that it had to be someone that Link knew, someone he'd willingly open the door for, someone he'd even have made the supreme sacrifice of providing with Maker's Mark." I nodded solemnly. "That could be a lot of people I'll admit, but you're one of them."

He shrugged noncommittally. "So was T.J.," he said. He moved slightly away from me, watching me all of the time. He went up onto the podium, where the speaker stood during the day. From up there he could see all of the room, see that none of the electrical equipment was on so that the microphones weren't picking us up, and know if anyone tried to come in from the outside halls. He looked it over, eyed me carefully again, inspected the room, with its empty desks and chairs. Nothing set him off, but he was nervous.

"Yeah," I said soothingly. "T.J.'s the logical choice. He was out with Link that night. Link was carrying anti-pollution and T.J. had to beat it for his bread and butter. Then I know that T.J. arranged to have Fred Olean kidnaped. He was

166

willing to do about anything." I nodded carefully. "Some things get in my way with T.J. though. He was already drunk, according to witnesses, when he brought Link back to the hotel. Whoever was in Link's room drank with him and I doubted that T.J. had any capacity left. But it was possible. But there was another thing I just couldn't believe in." I shook my head. "I couldn't believe that Link would use his own money to buy booze for a lobbyist or, even if he would have bought it, gone down for the liquor personally. Lobbyists are beasts of burden. But Link did use his own money and did do the running. He went down to the bar and got a twenty out of his own billfold and gave it all to the bartender. That's a pretty good tip and it was foreign to Link's nature to tip." I looked away for a minute and then back. He was watching me carefully. "Besides, if T.J. was desperate enough to kill Link then I thought he'd maybe have tried something pretty harsh with me. All I ever got was a botched-up kidnap plot. Then he went over the steps and that put him back in front of me as a real suspect. I wanted badly for it to be him. It would have cleaned it all up. It was awfully hard for me to believe in T.J. as a suicide, try as I might. He'd been in prison for a killing and he hadn't suicided, he'd had the guts to come here and lobby and know that someday he might get caught. T.J. just wasn't very suicidal as far as I was concerned. And the method he used wasn't a very likely method."

He stood in the podium almost negligently, hand down and out of sight. He said: "It wasn't me, Don. I swear to you. Nothing about this is going to make me say it was me." He watched me with uncertainty. "I wonder if it's safe to talk here?" he asked. "There's a night watchman, but he usually sleeps."

"You noticed too," I said. "Even when he's awake I doubt

167

he checks this wing. We'd hear him coming. Relax, friend. I'm not trying to get you to admit anything. I just want you to know how I got where I am and why I'm putting the bite on you." I shrugged. "All this makes no difference. Just listen. You don't have to talk." I stopped for a minute. "But Link was something, wasn't he? The complete representative?"

He nodded reluctantly.

"He knew the rules, observed the etiquette of the pecking order, respected the legislative hierarchy, carried out his political assignments, voted as the party desired on those things that were platform promises. He was a product of the system and loyal to it."

"Sure," he said, unable to resist. "And crooked like you and me."

"Maybe he was," I said. "But not for peanuts."

He looked at me coolly. "You talk as if there's a difference between taking a big money bribe to get something done and taking a tiny little bribe."

I smiled at him. "You and I had better decide there is a difference," I said.

He grinned. "Go on then," he said.

"What I'm trying to get at is that there were damn few people around that Link would have bought booze for. That was kind of important to me. I thought he might have bought booze for me, for example, but he'd surely have sent me after it. I'm a freshman representative and if booze was to be fetched I can bet you that I'd wind up doing the fetching. Maybe he'd have bought for a good friend and he might have bought for a woman—maybe Gertrude May." I shook my head. "I never could seriously believe it was her. She had motive and opportunity, but I couldn't believe that Link would have let her in the room. He'd spent the evening running each time he saw her. He ran early at the Bank-lobby room and he ran late, when he went down to the bar to pick up his booze. Besides, Gert was in love with him. And also Link had already turned down one girl, younger and more attractive than Gert that night. That got me back to three major possibles. That would be Link's three top legislative buddies. I hated to believe it, but it had to be that way."

"Maybe McGuire?" he asked, interested now. "I heard they had sort of a fight that night."

I shook my head. "Not McGuire. McGuire had too much to lose. He wants to run for the U. S. Senate. He's had political trouble before. He knows what it can mean to be under suspicion of doing something really wrong. Maybe he wanted, momentarily, to try Link early that evening, but even if he had, it would have been in a fit of rage. And it blew over and they were friendly later. McGuire could have been putting on an act, but things that happened later made me think not. He knew that T. J. Toy had faked his application for a lobbying permit and was a parole violator from another state, but he went along with Captain Carlson when Carlson wanted to wait a few days and keep an eye on Toy to see what was going to happen. I thought if McGuire had been the killer he'd have wanted T.J. picked up so that the finger would be dead on him and the investigation be halted."

"I didn't know you had any secret meeting with McGuire and Carlson," he said.

"No. I quit telling you about things around then. Both of you. Later, when T.J. went over the steps I thought Speaker McGuire was in very bad taste, but all he could figure anything on now and then was what it meant to his bid to run for the Senate."

I stopped and watched him. He was leaning against the podium front watching me intently.

"That just left the two of you," I said. "By that time I'd

decided from things I heard that someone had killed Link because Link was trying to raise some money out of a bill. I kept hearing he was going to quit. I kept hearing he was going to Florida. I knew him well enough to know that he couldn't have gone without some money. At first I thought he was trying to get it out of anti-pollution, but I couldn't see anyone with as much legislative ability as Link had fooling seriously with T.J. If it'd been anti-pollution then I was sure in my mind that Link would have had T.J. out of the house and away from the floor within an hour of the time he became involved. For every vote that T.J. bought, or thought he bought, he lost two. He was a walking scandal. I've seen legislators around him. I never saw anyone who looked comfortable. So I got to figuring that anti-pollution was only a figurehead. The money was elsewhere. I thought the idea was to vote out anti-pollution and another bill at the same time, make them so they came up for vote about the same time, so that anti-pollution could pass and everyone feel righteous about beating dirty little T.J. and the other bill not feel any heat at all. That second bill was cross-state power. I didn't know much about it, but I figured it could be big and quiet money."

"That's Chapell's bill," he said softly. "Sure I'm interested, but so's he."

"You're the guy who came to make the pay-off when I called," I said. "Chapell doesn't really need money, Ed. His wife is hooked on him and all he needs for luxury is to go home." I smiled. "Sometimes he doesn't do that well, but he manages often enough to keep her out of the divorce courts. And I've seen his wife and how she acts. She may hate the rest of us and she may be a real burning pain, but she does dote on George. Once she had the hots for Link, but that was a very long time ago and I couldn't find any tie between them now."

"They wouldn't advertise a tie," he said reasonably. "Maybe there was one and then Chapell found out about them. He could have killed Link because of it."

I shook my head. "No. It just wasn't that way. Gertrude told me something that I already knew, but hadn't realized. Link had a big thing in his head about youth. His own teeth were long, but he wanted youth around him. He wouldn't have fooled with Mrs. Chapell." I gave him a long look. "It was you, Ed."

His face was defiant. "Why?" he asked. "You keep pushing at me, but I haven't heard anything that ties me in. All you know about me is that I want a bill and I'm willing to dicker around with you about some money. A crapshooter like you needs money, Don." He smiled suddenly and it was like sun coming out to disperse rain. "So this meeting makes us both a little crooked, like Link, but it's a crookedness that this Statehouse has seen before and will undoubtedly see again. Quit trying to make it more than that."

"All right," I said soothingly. "A few questions then: How come you didn't go to the funeral?"

He shrugged. "I don't like them much. I seldom go. You were willing to go for me and do my wailing. Besides, I had to meet with the state people and get Sloan's successor lined out, as you had occasion to find out later." He smiled. "I fail to see the significance."

"None, really," I said. "You told me about your meeting before. From what the Speaker's said I thought he was the one who did the picking. I think that you had little, if anything, to do with it."

He frowned. "A lot of people were involved. I never tried to take full credit for your appointment. I might have tried to use my knowledge of it and of you to get a few things done I wanted, but that was all. That's fair, Robak. We do that up here, you know."

"All right," I said. "I'm not anyways near done yet. The next thing that bugged me was the taking down of my notice on the meeting of my committee. I couldn't figure that T.J. did it. He wanted a meeting held, or at least had never indicated he didn't want one. You watched me chalk the notice on the blackboard and then you took it off."

He grinned. "I could lie, but I won't. Maybe you've even got a witness who saw me. So I'll admit it. So what? I rubbed the meeting off because I didn't want the power bill coming up in committee until I'd made some senate contacts on it. It's a legitimate trick to rub meeting notices from that blackboard. Surely, even a cub like you can't equate that into a murder?"

"Okay," I conceded. "I'm merely trying to show how I got to you. Rubbing out my meeting notice showed me that you'd take steps to get what you wanted."

"So?"

"So I found out that Link was doing all of this planning about retirement. He had your bill in his committee. He must have seen, very early, how much you wanted it. From things he said the night he died I figured he had the arm on someone for half a million dollars, which could have made him a permanent vacationer, like the guy who built this Statehouse addition. Half a million would have been minor to a group of power companies that could build across a state line and raid top power users in this state. Hundreds of millions and maybe even billions of dollars were involved. Then, when I called you and put on the big bite, you came right away, Ed. And I knew you'd killed him when you came in that door."

He waited.

"Link was an old country boy," I said. "He'd never been around much, never taken a vacation. His idea of living was to come down here for the yearly sessions, then go back home and rest up, or maybe it was vice versa. This year there was a difference. Link wanted something more. He wanted out. He wanted away from this winter land. I think he figured that T.J. couldn't raise the kind of money to really put Link down South in style. So then he put it to you. T.J. had too much of a taint on him. Even if T.J. could have raised the kind of money that Link wanted, I think Link figured that big trouble might follow. Anti-pollution was too hot. If he did a swan dive on it and killed it after putting it up, he figured maybe that someone might get real, real interested and he couldn't believe that T.J. wouldn't fold if the heat was put on him. But you were a different matter. You don't have any taint to you, no smell. So he put the hand out to you. And I think you agreed or at least you pretended to agree." I nodded to myself. "I think Link wanted the money in advance. That's the only way to play. Promises to do something in the future sometimes don't get paid off. You made the arrangements to pay him sometime earlier that night, maybe when you saw him out at the black-and-tan place. It wouldn't have taken much—a wink—a gesture. So, later, you went to his room. You're the majority leader. He'd have gone out to get booze for you or McGuire. I didn't even know if he'd have gone for Chapell. Chapell's opposition. Going to get it for you was being a part of what he was, a part of his being a good legislator. You wanted him drunk, so you let him go, knowing he'd tell no one you were there because he wouldn't want anyone to know what was going on any more than you would. So you had a few more belts and he passed out. All of us knew he did pass out from time to time. You were waiting for it. It was opportunity knocking and you'd hoped for it. Even if you'd been seen entering his room you could always claim you left before anything happened. So you beat his head in

173

with something you'd brought with you—maybe whatever it is that you've got in your hands now—then you dumped him out the window. In a way you were unlucky. He fell in such a way that they knew he'd been hit before he went out the window. But no one saw you, so you sat tight and played it by ear." I looked up at him. "Wasn't that the way it was, Ed?"

He shook his head at me and smiled. "Go on."

"You must have been petrified when the maid knocked at the door, but everything went off pretty well. You waited until you were sure she'd gone. You made your first big mistake then. Like many people who fit in your category, you're a compulsive straightener, a bug for neatness. You cleaned up the pile of bills that must have spilled over when you were dragging Link to the window. You were in a hurry, but you'd made a mess, so you got all of those in sight. Then you weren't sure they'd think it was suicide, what with the maid and all, so you took some of the bill copies to give them something else to think on, if they didn't believe the suicide. You went back to your room and no one saw you and you waited. Nothing happened and you were pretty confident by the next day. So confident you made a real big mistake, Ed."

His face had grown weary. "I still haven't heard a thing but your foolish conjecture," he said.

"Okay," I said, "then the clincher: You told George Chapell that Link was going to Florida. You told him that after Link was dead. No one could have known that. Link made the arrangements in secret after he saw you at the black-and-tan place that night. Only someone who saw him after he got back to the Blue Hotel and his room could have known he was going to Florida. He'd never even been before, so there was no past behavior you could have inferred from."

He shook his head unbelievingly. "You haven't got anything," he said. "No jury in the world would or could convict me on that sort of evidence and you know it."

"I'm not a jury and I'm not trying to convict you," I said reasonably. "All I'm trying to do is convince you of how I got here tonight and what I'm going to start spouting if I don't get a hundred thousand. Not five thousand and not ten. A hundred thousand. You can get it for me, Ed. I figure you've got the bite on someone in the power companies for a lot of money."

He nodded. "If you did tell it," he said, "it might be the end of everything. I don't want the end yet. I don't think you'd convince anyone with a story that weak, but it could hurt me." He looked down at me and began to sentence me with his cold eyes. "It might hurt the party, too. Did you think about that, Robak?"

"Get me the hundred thousand," I said. "I'm letting you off easier than Link would have."

He smiled his sunny, meaningless smile. "I keep wondering if that would be the end of it once you had your hundred thousand. It's hard to stop shaking a money tree. Link was old. He promised to take the money and run with it and I believed him. Half a million. It was too much money."

"I figure it was half of what you had going," I said.

His eyes flickered and I knew I was right.

"You're still young," he said. "You're going to be around for a while. You start that story and they'll watch me from now on. Maybe it would hurt me bad enough so that I'd lose something I'd want." He calculated me with his eyes, adding and subtracting. Outside someone blew a horn loudly and he jumped and then relaxed.

I said: "I'll never be back again, Ed. Where I come from it's a real miracle I was here this once. You get me the money and I'll never say anything. I won't have to say anything, I promise. I'll take the money and I'll feed it in slow. It'll make the difference between steak and hamburger for the rest of my life." I stopped, seeing I wasn't adding anything to his computations. He'd added me up to a zero.

The hand came out of the pocket. It held a large gun, big enough to have been the weapon that bashed in Link's head. He held it on me, his eyes alert. "Too big a chance, Robak," he said. "Even if they didn't believe you then maybe someone would think it worth while to check out the others. There was another up home that I'm still sweating out. I got some money out of him—money I don't even need with what's coming now. Then there were two others down here. Everyone thought they were suicides. Link was the first one that didn't go smooth. He woke up and I had to hit him." He smiled without humor. "Later, I was thinking about maybe adding McGuire. This one up home was a doctor. I got some stuff from him I could put in McGuire's scotch. They'd think he'd just popped an overloaded blood vessel in his head or something. Then I'd have been the heir apparent." He eyed me wistfully, as if wondering where it had gone wrong for him and sorry about it. "I want his place in the scheme of things. It should be me they're talking about running for senator, not him. Why should it be that fat bastard?"

"I'll never say anything," I said again. "I told you I'd never have to tell."

He puzzled over that, pointing the gun at me all of the time.

"Let's go," he said finally. "We're going to take your car."

I nodded, hating him. He'd used anyone and anything for his own advantage. He'd lived his neat life without feeling or desire except for those things that benefited him. He was antiseptic and twisted and I'd seen one like him before. A long time before. I'd been appointed to defend that one.

Pure sociopath. Not technically insane, but prepared to do whatever needed to be done to upgrade himself to that next tenuous step on the ladder, where everything would certainly be all right, but never was. Nothing inside for the world around him, nothing inside but cunning and hurt for all of the world he came in contact with—but clever—able to conceal it. Hard to find out, never truthful except when it couldn't hurt.

It couldn't hurt him now.

"Link told me once that you were sharp," I said. "I suppose he meant sharp enough to cut a throat. It was a phrase he liked to use."

He mused, almost planning it. "Tomorrow they'll find you in your car. It'll look like you had to stop someplace along a deserted road and . . ."

"Tell me why you killed T.J."

He stopped for a minute and frowned with annoyance. "I heard they were looking for him over the late news. I guessed why. I knew where he was, so I called him and told him what was going on. He wanted to get out of the state. I picked him up in my car and took him to the Statehouse. I told him I could help—that I had some connections that could fix it all. I thought if he was dead and you had the note that it would all be ended." The muscles in his arms and neck corded again. "I picked him up and dropped him over the stairs." He smiled. "I used the typer in your office for the note." He looked around again. His voice was very gentle. "Come on now. Let's go."

"No," I said.

He shrugged and raised the gun. "I'll shoot you here then. It isn't as good, but it'll have to do. By the time the night watchman gets here, even if he hears it, I'll be long gone."

"How about my witnesses?" I asked.

177

He shook his head. "No. You needed the money, Robak. You're a crook, just like Link. You didn't tell anyone."

"Want to meet them?" I asked.

His eyes watched me without comprehension.

I tapped the top of the desk with a hard fist and looked around. In the rear of the chamber the seats came around. The lovely chairs that looked the same fore and aft. In the first and nearest was Captain Carlson. He sat cross-legged in it and he had a big gun also. It was pointed unwaveringly at Ed Polsen. Across the room I saw little Harlan Hill, his thin, black face digesting the sight of evil where it had not been expected. Away from him, near the far door, there was another state policeman. He also had a gun. My partner made a fourth spectator. He sat all hunched, his face gray. As a past state senator he knew what was going to happen. Olean was the last one. All of them watched Polsen.

"I had them get in the chairs, Ed," I said. "Then they turned around. The chairs look the same, front or back." Then I said, because I hated him very much and wanted him to know that he'd missed something and it had put him into this situation. "I guess you never noticed them. This cub did. So you learn something new every session."

For just a moment his eyes flickered and I thought he was going to take his chances and shoot me. But then he calculated the matter with his sociopathic mind. He'd never been caught before and maybe . . .

He put the gun on the podium. "A joke," he said. "I knew they were out there all of the time." He sounded like the kid who's been left out of the story, the one forced to the fringes of the crowd, uninvited, holding the bag for the snipe that never appear.

"Let's see how much they laugh, Ed," I said gravely.

They took him away.

CHAPTER XV

Much later, near the end of the session, I went over to the Law-lobby rooms one night and had too much to drink, something I was doing more and more.

The party was in full bloom that night. My partner, former Senator Adams, was there. So was Fred Olean, who'd brought a copy of the Capitol City *Enquirer*. He showed me a story in the middle pages. Ed Polsen had issued a new statement proclaiming his innocence, hinting at a conspiracy against him by powerful figures, and promising sensational developments, all from the confines of the Capitol City jail.

"You tricked him, Robak," Olean said, and smiled. "He had his bond hearing last week and was turned down on that. It looks like he's going to have to stay in jail until the trial. He got some lawyer out of New York who wears his hair shoulder length." He nodded. "That lawyer says his statements made that night in the chamber are inadmissible."

179

I shrugged and looked around the room for the familiar face I'd lost, but she wasn't there and hadn't been there since that night I'd had my meeting with Polsen.

I said: "I'm afraid, for Ed's sake, that it'll be a trick the Supreme Court will allow."

He smiled again. "I can still remember sitting there with my legs pulled up in that chair. I thought you were full of it right up to the time he started talking about killing people, killing you."

He watched me re-examine the crowd. "You ever find out where Judy went?"

I shook my head. "It got obvious that she'd moved to get away from me. So I quit looking after a while."

"Pride won't keep you warm at night." He nodded, and not at me. "I remember," he added softly.

For a while we didn't look at each other and we sat there and sipped our drinks. Senator Adams watched with interest as two of his senate compatriots of past years did push-ups in a far corner of the room for some alcoholic reason. He watched them and he watched me and I thought I saw a hint of worry in his eyes.

He said: "I've a copy of the student underground newspaper I brought up from Bington. I'll give it to you sometime. You were right there in favor, treated as handsomely as a four-letter word. If you run again I'll bet you get ten per cent of the student primary vote. Tuition raise is dead, anti-pollution is on the governor's desk and he's promised to sign it."

I said: "They were using those two bills. Maybe it didn't begin that way, but it worked out. The tuition raise and anti-pollution were useful diversions, meant to draw heat. Cross-state power would benefit because it wasn't as controversial as the other bills. And the two hot bills could be used to trade for votes for the power bill if needed. That's how I got Harlan Hill to sit in one of those chairs that night, by pointing out that he and his kids were being used to take the heat off another bill. And no one in the know cared if there were riots, cared that the tuition bill was unfair, or cared whether or not we needed anti-pollution."

The senator sat hunched in his chair. He had blossomed here in Capitol City. In the uncertain light of the room his face seemed young and unlined.

"They were two of a kind," I said. "Link and Polsen. You told me something about Polsen early that should have set me off. You told me you caught him in a lie in a trial, but couldn't get him to change his story. When I got to thinking about it, thinking about him then he reminded me of someone I'd known once. A thief I had had examined by psychiatrists at the state hospital. Alan Welch. Maybe you remember him? Very lovely and glib and bright. The psychiatrists said he was legally sane. Police caught him in the act of burglary and I got appointed to defend him. The psychiatrists testified that he knew he was doing wrong, could stop himself from the act with ease, but just didn't feel that anyone else was bright enough to catch him or convict him." I sighed. "A sociopath then. An explanation for everything and no backing from a caught lie. He thought the jury was in his hand right up to the moment they found him guilty. Then, of course, it became my fault. He's still writing letters to the state bar association about me from prison. Polsen reminded me of him. The world was made for Polsen. No one else has value. If we hadn't caught him, he'd have been at it right now, smiling his way upward and onward, disposing of whoever got in the way." I nodded to myself. "But wasn't that Link also? Anyway, when I saw how it was progressing I stopped reporting back what was going on. Chapell was hostile to the idea of an investigation and Polsen was using me to determine what he needed to do. He could watch what was going on and then determine his steps."

"Captain Carlson said they found some traces of blood and hair on the butt of that big gun he held on you. They match with Link's."

I nodded. I'd heard it before.

Across the room I spied George Chapell. He was in close touch with a red-headed young lady. His eyes caught mine and I nodded, but maybe he didn't see me. Anyway, he didn't nod back.

"There's a good man," I said to Fred. "He'll chase anything as long as his wife isn't watching."

"Maybe an anonymous letter," Fred said, smiling to take some of the intent out of it.

The senator smiled at him. "The political implications seem nil, despite the publicity in the Capitol City *Enquirer*. The bad seems about balanced by the good, seeing as how you caught him."

I raised a hand in the air and reminded: "Aided by the stanch help of Speaker McGuire." In the stories we'd released to the news media McGuire had always been a confidant, a planner. His Senate campaign was proceeding at a quickening rate. I didn't envy him, thinking of all of those chicken suppers I'd had to go through in just one county. Three million hands to be wrung for McGuire, cold peas and *no* drinking.

I looked at my own glass, reminded. Surprisingly it was still half-full and I had a sip.

I said, remembering: "I knew if I let him name places that he'd come up with the legislative chamber. I think he met T.J. there. I kept finding fault with every other place he named and gave him no place I named that he could accept. So, eventually, he named the chamber."

Someone had brought a large supply of Polish sausage and cooked it there in the Law-lobby rooms. Around me people were eating the sausage and I watched them.

Somehow I didn't really blame Judy for not coming back, for having an unlisted number, and for moving without goodbye. I'd frightened her. Life had already made her a bit afraid and along I'd come and deepened the fear.

And so she was gone.

So what?

The jukebox played and I quit listening to conversation and just sat there brooding in dark silence until Olean nudged me sharply.

I looked up and saw what he wanted me to see.

She came in the door and took the proffered drink and looked shyly around and found me. I got up shakily and went across the room, feeling my drinks. I took her hand.

"I wasn't going to . . ." she began.

I said, all in a rush: "It's all right."

She looked up at me and I took her hand and led her to the tiny dance floor where a few couples were dancing. The music was soft and in that moment of coming together I knew that Judy was all right now, without fear, and that maybe, just maybe, I was too.